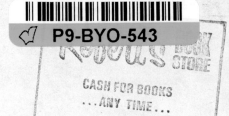
THE COQUETTE

HANNAH WEBSTER FOSTER was born in Salisbury, Massachusetts, on September 10, 1758. Her father, Grant Webster, was a prosperous Boston merchant. After her mother, Hannah Wainwright Webster, died in 1762, she was sent to boarding school. Although she wrote one of the best-selling novels of the early national period and a work widely regarded, even in its own time, as one of the finest early American novels, Foster, like most women writers of that era, has been largely passed over by social and literary history. Little is known of her adult life except that in 1785 she married the Reverend John Foster, a graduate of Dartmouth College and pastor of the First Church in Brighton, Massachusetts, and that she wrote two novels, *The Coquette; or, The History of Eliza Wharton* (1797) and *The Boarding School; or, Lessons of a Preceptress to Her Pupils* (1798). She also bore six children, including two daughters who would become popular writers of the nineteenth century, Harriet Vaughan Cheney and Eliza Lanesford Cushing. Foster went to live with the latter in Montreal during her old age and died there on April 17, 1840.

CATHY N. DAVIDSON is Professor of English at Michigan State University. A recipient of Guggenheim and Woodrow Wilson fellowships, she has published many articles and books, including *Revolution and the Word: The Rise of the Novel in America* and an edition of early America's best-selling novel, Susanna Haswell Rowson's *Charlotte Temple*.

THE
COQUETTE

HANNAH WEBSTER FOSTER

Edited with
an Introduction by
CATHY N. DAVIDSON

OXFORD UNIVERSITY PRESS
New York Oxford

Oxford University Press

Oxford New York Toronto
Delhi Bombay Calcutta Madras Karachi
Petaling Jaya Singapore Hong Kong Tokyo
Nairobi Dar es Salaam Cape Town
Melbourne Auckland

and associated companies in
Beirut Berlin Ibadan Nicosia

First American edition of *The Coquette,* 1797
This paperback edition, with new editorial matter, first published

198 Madison Avenue, New York, New York 10016-4314

LIBRARY OF CONGRESS CATALOGING-IN-PUBLICATION DATA
Foster, Hannah Webster, 1759–1840.
The coquette.
Bibliography: p. I. Davidson, Cathy N., 1949– . II. Title.
PS744.F7C6 1986 813'.2 86-18001
ISBN 0-19-504239-5 (pbk.)

16 18 19 17 15
Printed in the United States of America

CONTENTS

INTRODUCTION

When a thirty-seven-year-old woman came to the Bell Tavern in Danvers (now Peabody), Massachusetts, gave birth to a stillborn child, and then followed that child to her own death on July 25, 1788, she and her tragic demise soon became the subject of national attention. Long before Hannah Webster Foster turned these events into *The Coquette; or, The History of Eliza Wharton; A Novel; Founded on Fact* (1797), Elizabeth Whitman's life and death had already been transformed into a sensational story, as is evident in even the first published account which appeared in the *Salem Mercury* for July 29, 1788.* Purportedly written by one Captain Goodhue, the landlord of the Bell Tavern, this first notice effectively balances asserted propriety (she was waiting for her husband) and suggested scandal (did she really have one?):

> Last Friday, a female stranger died at the Bell Tavern, in Danvers; and on Sunday her remains were decently interred. The circumstances relative to this woman are such as excite curiosity, and interest our feelings. She was brought to the Bell in a chaise . . . by a young man whom she had engaged for that purpose. . . . She remained at this inn till her death, in expectation of the arrival of her husband, whom she expected to come for her, and appeared anxious at his delay. She was averse to being interrogated concerning herself or connexions; and kept much retired to her chamber, employed in needlework, writing, etc. . . . Her conversation, her writings and her manners, bespoke the advantage of a re-

*A fuller discussion of this novel and the social context in which it was written can be found in Chapter 6 of *Revolution and the Word: The Rise of the Novel in America* (New York: Oxford University Press, 1986).

spectable family and good education. Her person was agreeable; her deportment, amiable and engaging; and, though in a state of anxiety and suspense, she preserved a cheerfulness which seemed to be not the effect of insensibility, but of a firm and patient temper.

Within days the account was picked up and reprinted by the *Massachusetts Centinel* and then in dozens of other newspapers throughout New England. It was the stuff of good rumor, of gossip, of sentimental fiction.

What led to the "Elizabeth Whitman mystery"? Given the late eighteenth century's notably high incidence of both illegitimacy and maternal mortality, surely many another woman had borne a child out of wedlock and died of puerperal fever. But as even the above report suggests, the essential appeal of this story was its contradictory nature. To start with, what was a nice woman like Elizabeth Whitman doing in a place like that and in that condition? Miss Whitman was the daughter of a highly respected minister, the Reverend Elnathan Whitman. On her mother's side, she was descended from the Stanley family that had governed Connecticut almost from its colonial beginnings. She was also related to the Jonathan Edwards family, to Aaron Burr, and to the poet John Trumbull. Two of her suitors had been Yale preceptors. She had corresponded regularly with Joel Barlow. Hartford's highest society knew and respected her for her wit, her intelligence, and her charm. Yet she died in a tavern, seduced and abandoned, a fate right out of the popular eighteenth-century novels that vociferously warned against just that fate. Nor were the novels the only texts bearing on the matter of her demise. Once Whitman's identity was revealed, ministers, journalists, and freelance moralists industriously made *meaning*—their meaning—of her otherwise perplexing end. In the redaction of an anonymous essayist in the (Boston) *Independent Chronicle* of September 11, 1788, for example, Elizabeth Whitman's life and death become, simply, "a good moral lecture to young ladies."

By the time Hannah Webster Foster published her novel in 1797, the Elizabeth Whitman story had become well known in the new nation, an object lesson on the dangers of female rights and female liberty. The whole question of just what role women should have in the new country was being vigorously debated as America worked out its own definition of democracy. Would women win their independence too? The novel, as a literary form that especially addressed women, raised several controversial issues—female education, female employment, political and legal rights of women, and the double sexual standard. The Whitman story, however, subordinated all other feminist issues to that last one, which was also a key social issue of the day. Indeed, the era's governing assumption that lost virginity proved, for a woman, lost worth mandated such attention. Elizabeth Whitman had to become The Fallen Woman. For many writing at the time, the lesson was simple. All that needed to be said about her character was that she had lost it.

The early accounts of Elizabeth Whitman's decline and fall also served the dual purpose of criticizing any intellectual pretensions that a woman might possess and of condemning the novel as a new literary form which particularly fostered just such pretensions in its women readers while simultaneously sanctioning any promptings toward licentiousness. Elizabeth Whitman becomes, in these renderings, a case study of a woman first misled by her education into a taste for novels and then corrupted through indulging that unwholesome appetite. In fact, William Hill Brown in the first American novel—his anonymously published *The Power of Sympathy: Or, The Triumph of Nature. Founded in Truth* (1789), a work which he pointedly did not call a novel— invokes the fate of Elizabeth Whitman to warn, duplicitously, against novel reading: "She was a great reader of novels and romances and having imbibed her ideas of *the characters of men*, from those fallacious sources, became vain and coquetish, and rejected several offers of marriage, in expectation of receiving one more agreeable to her fanciful idea." It was the official view.

Brown merely borrows the verdict delivered in the *Massachusetts Centinel* on September 20, 1788: "She was *a great reader of romances,* and having formed her notions of happiness from that corrupt source, became vain and coquetish." Thus was a learned and accomplished woman translated into a poor, pathetic victim of fiction whose dishonor and death could be partly redeemed only by serving to save others from a similar end.

To turn that well-known scandal and accepted story into one of the most reprinted early American novels, Hannah Webster Foster had to reread this protagonist and her plight. The fact of her fall is not altered but the significance of that fact is. In the prescriptive literature, the tragic end of Elizabeth Whitman clearly points out the different course she should have followed. However, the same end for the fictional character raises serious questions about the choices with which she was presented. Foster's Eliza sees the virtues and the faults of both of her suitors and recognizes that neither man would make, for her, a suitable husband. Yet she is not strong enough to reject them both and perhaps become the socially stigmatized "spinster." Displeased with her choices, unable to accept the alternative of a single life, she vacillates indecisively throughout most of the novel, timorous and bold, aware and self-deceived, loudly proclaiming her own independence and ever accommodating to the strictures of others. Nor are the suitors simple stereotypes either. The Reverend Boyer is partly a respected clergyman, partly a pious fraud. He voices spiritual values and he is also preeminently concerned with the figure he cuts in the world and in his own estimation. Major Sanford, admittedly, is vain and selfish. But he is intelligent, articulate, and he can treat Eliza seriously, especially when he talks to her of Boyer's limitations. More surprising, although he does little to prove it, Sanford is, in his way, in love with Eliza, whereas the Reverend Boyer appears somewhat calculating in his pursuit of a proper wife who will suit his station and his profession. If the facts give us the choice that the protagonist did make, the fiction gives us all the right reasons for that wrong choice.

Foster's novel reading of Elizabeth Whitman's story remains, of course, founded in fact. Several historical characters, for example, underwent name changes while retaining the same initials, which suggests an intentional blurring of the division between fiction and fact and an invitation to the reader to enjoy that same blurring. Two of Whitman's suitors, the Reverend Joseph Howe (whom her parents originally chose for their daughter but who died before the marriage could take place) and the Reverend Joseph Buckminster (who subsequently sought her hand), are slightly fictionalized into the Reverends Haly and Boyer. Historical personages have also been advanced as the originals for the protagonist's women friends, and for her seducer "Peter Sanford" as well. By the mid-nineteenth century, Pierrepont Edwards (son of Jonathan Edwards) was generally assumed to be the model for Major Sanford. Other candidates for the honor have also been proposed: Aaron Burr, New York State Senator James Watson, Joel Barlow, and an unnamed "French nobleman" whose parents objected to his "secret marriage" to a Protestant minister's daughter from Connecticut. But all such possibilities remain conjecture, and part of the appeal of the novel is the continuing question of the real identity of the seducer. Although Whitman left a cache of poems and letters at her death, none identifies her lover by any name other than the pathetically ironic pseudonym "Fidelio." And if Hannah Webster Foster knew (she was remotely connected to the scandal—the Reverend John Foster, Hannah's husband, was a first cousin of the wife of Elizabeth Whitman's father's cousin), she wasn't telling.

Foster's handling of historical material is particularly remarkable for the way in which she continually added complexity even to the small details that had routinely devolved into stereotypes in the earlier accounts of Elizabeth Whitman. None of these, for example, credit the female protagonist with a rational weighing of a prospective husband's qualifications, despite the fact that her second suitor, the Reverend Buckminster, was well known in his day as a man subject to prolonged fits of depression and outbursts of uncontrolled temper. "She refused two as good of-

fers of marriage as she deserved," avers the *Independent Chronicle* of September 11, 1788, "because she aspired higher than to be a clergyman's wife; and having coquetted till past her prime, fell into criminal indulgences." Foster transforms this reductionist account of Elizabeth's anti-clericalism and social climbing and looks at Eliza's determination to make her marriage an egalitarian match based on mutual affection. A clergyman's wife herself, Foster well knew just what that employment entailed and, more to the point, her fictional Eliza, the daughter of a minister's wife, also knows the prerequisites for the position and knows, too, she does not fit the bill. As she admits to her mother, "My disposition is not calculated for that sphere. There are duties arising from the station, which I fear I should not be able to fulfill; cares and restraints to which I could not submit" (p. 39). Having narrowly escaped one loveless marriage through the fortuitous death of the fiancé imposed upon her by the "shackles" of "parental authority" (p. 13), she is determined to marry in the future only if reason and fancy, her mind and her heart, are both engaged.

Socially conservative readers may well have intimated the seeds of Eliza's downfall in this daughter's belated declaration of independence and her egalitarian concept of marriage. Foster, however, takes considerable pains to affirm her protagonist's ideals. When early in the novel she leaves her mother's home in which she was immured with her dying clergyman fiancé, she goes to visit her friends, the Richmans. Their marriage embodies the ideal of egalitarian partnership then advocated by such feminist thinkers as the British Mary Wollstonecraft or the American Judith Sargent Murray. It is Eliza's ideal too. Her "heart approved and applauded" her friends' happiness. Her tragedy is not that she set her sights too high but that she encounters no equivalent of General Richman. What she is offered, instead, is a difficult choice between unsatisfactory alternatives, a common quandary in early American sentimental novels and a dilemma no doubt faced by many young American women.

The Coquette, then, is not simply an allegory of seduction. The

shift in genre from sermon to novel in the Whitman/Wharton narrative entails a concomitant transformation of focus and philosophy. Set within a specific context of limiting marriage laws and restrictive social mores, the novel is not so much a story of the wages of sin as a study of the wages of marriage. Marriage reduced a woman to a *feme covert* [*sic*], literally a "hidden woman" legally consigned to the not always magnanimous rule of her husband. Foster knew this. In the realistic world of her fictional account, virtue and virtuous women are not always rewarded. Thus Sanford's lawfully wedded wife, a woman shown to be honest, admirable, and attractive, fares almost as disastrously as Eliza. She is ruined financially by her marriage to Sanford; her child, too, is stillborn. Furthermore, even Mrs. Richman, the epitome of republican motherhood in the novel, cannot be permanently happy within her familial sphere. "All my happiness is centered within the limits of my own walls; and I grudge every moment that calls me from the pleasing scenes of domestic life" (p. 97), she writes, soon after the birth of her daughter—who soon afterward dies. This death is a definite tempering of the joys of domesticity and another realistic reflection of the age with its notably high rates of infant and maternal mortality.

If marriage meant everything—legally, socially, and emotionally—in a woman's life, on what grounds did she make that crucial decision? By fictionalizing the lives of the women who surround Eliza, Foster provided her early readers with an opportunity to see women very much like themselves, women who also had to make decisions about the course of their lives. As the women within the novel exchange views and ideas on such crucial subjects as friendship, marriage, and economic security, their letters constitute a dialogue in which the reader is also invited to participate, if only vicariously. For its first audience particularly, *The Coquette* thereby presented a remarkably detailed assessment of the marital possibilities facing late eighteenth-century women of the middle or upper-middle classes.

Crucial questions for just such women are asked and dramatized in the text. What were their choices? What kinds of behav-

ior would promote or prevent certain matches? And how do men view the whole matter of courtship and marriage? Because she wrote in the epistolary mode, Foster was able to provide a particularly revealing assessment of that last question. Men in this novel, as well as women, speak in their own voice, and the reader is allowed to eavesdrop on what each sex says when the other is not listening. On that last score, the twelve letters that Sanford sends his friend, Charles Deighton, provide a telling example of male discourse in contrast to female discourse, and Sanford effectively voices the self-justifying evasions, the hypocrisy, and the overt misogyny of the seducer—all of which he skillfully conceals in his conversations with Eliza. We as readers see what she does not: how glibly he puts on the mask of concerned friendship when he addresses Eliza; how easily he slips it off when he writes, cynically, to Deighton about the progress he is making toward his intended sexual conquest. Similarly, the nine letters exchanged between the Reverend Boyer and his friend, Selby, demonstrate the self-serving assumptions of these respectable men about natural female subservience, and the dicta in their letters on the whole duty of women bear out Eliza's worst apprehensions about the restricted life that would be hers if she were to marry Boyer and become a clergyman's wife.

The bulk of the novel, however, is "woman-talk": women confiding, advising, chiding, warning, disagreeing, misleading, confronting, and consoling each other. A full two-thirds of the seventy-four letters that comprise *The Coquette* are written by women to women, and not always about the men in their lives. Eliza, especially, exhibits in her discourse the ideas and aspirations of a *feme sole*—the independent, unmarried woman. In contrast to that state is the status of Eliza's close friend and most regular correspondent, Lucy Freeman, who in the course of the novel marries to become Mrs. Sumner. As a married woman, she can no longer be so free as she formerly was with her time or attention. To quote Eliza: "Marriage is the tomb of friendship. It appears to me a very selfish state. Why do people, in general, as soon as they are married, centre all their cares, their concerns,

and pleasures in their own families? Former acquaintances are neglected or forgotten. The tenderest ties between friends are weakened, or dissolved; and benevolence itself moves in a very limited sphere" (p. 24). "Women's sphere" is here aptly portrayed as "very limited"—a closed and enclosing concern for a husband's well-being—which gives us one of the earliest fictional critiques of the "cult of domesticity," a nineteenth-century ideology that insisted that, although women had no official political status, they did enjoy sovereignty within the ultimately more important domain, the home. Foster early in the novel asks if so limited a freedom is really any freedom after all.

The Coquette, however, does not openly challenge the basic structure of patriarchal culture but, instead, exposes its fundamental injustices through the details and disasters of the plot. Consider, for example, how, after the Reverend Haly's death, Eliza's mother along with the young woman's female friends worry constantly about her marital prospects, for she does not have an inheritance of her own. They do not advise (much less prepare) her to earn a wage; they only urge her to obtain a husband who does. Yet her manifest talents—her beauty, her charm, her intelligence—constitute no negotiable capital in any matrimonial transaction. "Forgive my plainness," Eliza's friend, Lucy Freeman, writes of the Reverend Boyer. "His situation in life is, perhaps, as elevated as you have a right to claim" (p. 27). Neither does a fortune of one's own substantially alter one's station, as the example of Nancy Sanford amply attests. The wealthy woman, as much as the poor, is still dependent on a husband's good sense and goodwill. All women are thus potential paupers, married women especially so. But without a husband to provide for her and lacking the skills to earn her own living, a woman's situation can be as desperate as was the historical Elizabeth Whitman's at the Bell Tavern. At her death, the abandoned woman left 2 ginneys, 1 crown, and some paltry possessions (six silver spoons, three rings, a couple of dresses, handkerchiefs, ribbons, and caps; a writing case with paper and pens and sealing wafers; a few baby clothes). That sad inventory, in actual

and symbolic measure, movingly sums up an unmarried woman's social worth and final estate in the new Republic.

Other features of the society are also encapsulated in the novel. As Eliza fully realizes, when a woman marries a man, she must marry not only into his class but into his occupation as well. She anticipates being "completely miserable" as a minister's wife, and Sanford effectively reiterates those all too well-founded fears: "You are aware, I suppose, when you form a connection with that man, you must . . . content yourself with a confinement to the tedious round of domestic duties, the pedantic conversation of scholars, and the invidious criticisms of a whole town" (p. 50). Boyer, pompous and self-satisfied, attempts (the choice of words here is most appropriate) to "seduce [Eliza] into matrimony" by soberly expatiating on the advantages of being joined to such a man as himself. "He is," Eliza writes, "very eloquent upon the subject; and his manners are so solemn that I am strongly tempted . . . to laugh" (p. 66). And so is the reader. But Major Sanford is hardly an alternative. Witty and charming as he may be, he is also a thoroughgoing misogynist, and a thoroughly dishonest one at that. His letters to Deighton are filled with stupid and shallow remarks about the stupidity and shallowness of women. He insists, for example, that he can be "severe upon the sex" because he has "found so many frail ones among them"—as if he were a latter-day Diogenes searching for an honest woman. He also insists that if he seduces Eliza, the fault will be entirely hers. "She knows my character, and has no reason to wonder if I act consistently with it" (p. 56). Yet he has just implored her to "let the kind and lenient hand of friendship assist in directing my future steps" (p. 37), which is hardly the open avowal of his intentions that he subsequently and quite hypocritically pretends he has made.

What appear to Eliza as choices—alternative men and alternative lifestyles—are not choices at all. Yet by keeping her options open and considering her suitors, she advances no closer to the egalitarian marriage of the Richmans. We have, instead, opponents who cancel one another out and who, by implication, can-

cel out Eliza too. For each, she was mostly a prize and a proof of his own prowess. In each case more could be proved by discarding the prize than by claiming it. Eliza does finally decide to marry the minister but "was entangled by a promise" to tell Sanford first. When Boyer discovers his prospective bride in conversation with that rival, he storms from the scene. He will not hear Eliza's explanation, for his dashed hopes (he thinks) and offended vanity (we see) provide all the explanation he needs. Soon he is writing to renounce his love, to catalogue her various faults and failings, and all from pure "benevolence." Sanford is delighted by his success in destroying Eliza's chances with Boyer. Sanford also soon leaves town. He goes away "on business" promising to return in a few months but, a year later, he is still gone and in that whole time he has not once written to the woman he claimed to love. Eliza, faced not with a freedom of choice but an absence of suitors, begins to realize that she has been played for a fool—a truth brought home even more forcefully when Boyer announces his engagement to a suitably appreciative, suitably proper woman and when Sanford finally returns, having acquired, while away, both a wife and that wife's fortune. Eliza naively sought to exercise her freedom only to learn that she had none.

The course of that learning is crucial to the novel, for the genesis of Eliza's fall lies at least as much in the virtues of Boyer as in the vices of Sanford. When the clergyman first goes off in his terminal huff, Eliza well can wonder "whether [she] had sustained a real loss in Mr. Boyer's departure" (p. 93). But Sanford's subsequent departure, along with the continuing absence of any other official suitors, soon casts a different light on her first loss from which the second has followed. She must remain in the fishbowl of Hartford, scorned by those who knew all along that her flirtations, her decision to sow her "wild oats" before settling into the restricted role of the clergyman's wife, could only lead to disaster. Publicly humiliated by the way in which the town so obviously relishes and affirms her discomfiture, she is brought, partly through her failing spirits and partly through Mrs.

Richman's counsel, to reevaluate the Reverend's dubious charms. Her letter to him is all humility and self-abnegation, but perhaps the most poignant detail in this sad missive is her hope that, even if his "affections are entirely alienated or otherwise engaged," he still might consent to consider himself her friend. That last hope is as vain as all her others. Again Boyer writes to shower her with accusations before announcing his betrothal to "the virtuous, the amiable, the accomplished Maria Selby," and counseling Eliza to "adhere, with undeviating exactness, to the path of rectitude and innocence" (p. 104).

"Oh my friend, I am undone!" Eliza writes upon receiving Boyer's letter, using the precise words that in seduction novels typically signal a woman's fall. "His conduct," she continues with an even more loaded term, assures her "ruin. . . . By confessing my faults, and by avowing my partiality to him, I have given him the power of triumphing in my distress; of returning to my tortured heart all the pangs of slighted love! and what have I now to console me?" (p. 105). Three times Eliza voices the plaintive cry of the seduced woman. Soon thereafter, as if physically to confirm her psychologically fallen status, she enters into the affair with Sanford just as she also concomitantly sinks into physical infirmity and mental instability. At the same time, she becomes less present in the text—she writes fewer letters and is seen in society less often. Others now must recount the story that was once her own; the mode of its telling has been taken from her.

This negation of the female self—her freedoms, her possibilities—forms the basis of the sentimental plot, just as it informed the lives of a vast majority of the sentimental novel's readers. One effective method Foster employs to convey this demeaning of her central character is to have her literally render herself as she has been symbolically rendered by her society. At crucial junctures in the novel, Eliza *chooses* silence, but that narrative silence provides the subtext from which we can best read the protagonist's fall. Denied voice and will, she really cannot be seduced because, simply put, she has no say in the matter. Suc-

cumbing to Sanford merely confirms and symbolizes what rejection by Boyer has already proved. Sex is merely a half-sublimated suicide, a decline into a figurative death (a horrific rendition of "the little death") that prefigures her real one.

Eliza's silence also epitomizes an essential problem in the entire sentimental subgenre—a type of fiction written explicitly for women, often by women, but which does not in radical ways rewrite women's position within society. How does one grant a voice to a woman who, given the society in which the novel is written and read, enjoys neither voice nor privilege? More specifically, how can the life and death of Elizabeth Whitman emphasize meanings other than those already rendered into stereotypes and sexist clichés by the innumerable sermons, newspaper accounts, and didactic essays of the time? *The Coquette* and other eighteenth-century sentimental novels are ultimately about silence, subservience, and stasis (the accepted attributes of woman as traditionally defined) in contradistinction to conflicting impulses toward self-expression, independence, and action (the ideals of the new American nation). But what is the resolution of this central conflict? The problem arises because the form itself—or the writer—cannot imagine a life beyond her society's limitations without violating the essential social realism on which sentimental fiction (contrary to the usual critical clichés) is ultimately based. Eliza, for all the complexity of her motives and ambivalence of her actions, dies the same death that Elizabeth Whitman suffered.

In Hannah Webster Foster's novel, life does not suggest many unconventional choices. Even Mrs. Richman advocated Eliza's marriage to Boyer. Is marriage to a Boyer the best that an intelligent, well-educated woman can hope for, particularly when the alternative, Major Sanford, is no alternative at all? "What a pity," Eliza confides to her friend Lucy, "that the graces and virtues are not oftner united! They must, however, meet in the man of my choice; and till I find such a one, I shall continue to subscribe my name Eliza Wharton" (p. 22). She does, of course, precisely that. As Eliza Wharton she departs initially from her moth-

er's house and as Eliza Wharton still she departs finally and through death from the text of the novel, from the tragedy of her life, which hardly constitutes a vindication of the rights of women.

Eliza Wharton sins and dies. Her death can convey the conservative moral that many critics of the time demanded. Yet the circumstances of that death seem designed to tease the reader into thought. It is in precisely these interstices—the disjunctions between the conventional and radical readings of the plot—that the early American sentimental novel flourishes. It is in the irresolution of Eliza Wharton's dilemma that the novel, as a genre, differentiates itself from the solemn tracts on Elizabeth Whitman. Tracts readily prescribe just how a young woman should lead her life and make her marriage; they imply that virtuous choices will be rewarded with personal happiness. But in the realistic complexity of *The Coquette*, the equation between virtue and happiness breaks down. Where women lack the power to procure their own rewards, happiness, in marriages or affairs, depends largely on the luck of the draw. And where women have no social, political, or legal status except through their husbands, the deck is stacked irrevocably against the female player.

In *The Coquette*, Hannah Webster Foster calls the more conventionally grounded stories of Elizabeth Whitman into question. It is easy to avoid too much novel-reading. It is also easy to avoid social-climbing and an anti-clerical cast of mind. But how does one escape the social parameters of female powerlessness and female constraint? This question is left pointedly unanswered by the novelist. Only the reader can attempt to work out a better answer than the one Elizabeth Whitman and Eliza Wharton too late discovered.

CATHY N. DAVIDSON

NOTE ON THE TEXT

The text is printed from the American Antiquarian Society's copy of the first edition of *The Coquette; or, The History of Eliza Wharton; A Novel; Founded on Fact*, published anonymously (the title page indicates only that it is "By a Lady of Massachusetts") in 1797. Samuel Etheridge printed the novel for the Boston publisher and bookseller Ebenezer Larkin. The frontispiece facsimile of the title page from the 1797 edition appears through the courtesy of the American Antiquarian Society.

In this edition, the eighteenth-century "ſ" has been replaced by the modern "s," and minor misprints (arising from broken or missing letters or obvious typographical errors) have been silently corrected. However, the original edition has been kept intact as much as possible, including capitalization, grammatical, and punctuation practices which give some of the flavor of eighteenth-century writing. (The modern reader will be especially aware of the heavy use of semi-colons throughout and the omission of most quotation marks.) Commonplace eighteenth-century spellings have also been retained: for example, "apostacy" (apostasy), "chuse" (choose), "croud" (crowd), "dont" (don't), "desart" (desert), "envited" (invited), "exhilerated" (exhilarated), "extacy" (ecstasy), "fulfil" (fulfill), "inclose" (enclose), "intirely" (entirely), "manoeuvring" (maneuvering), "mislead" (misled), "oftner" (more often), "recal" (recall), "sagatious" (sagacious), "sooth" (soothe), "steping" (stepping), "to day" (today), and "to morrow" (tomorrow). Explanatory footnotes have been added in places, especially where meaning and usage have altered markedly since the novel's original publication.

SELECTED BIBLIOGRAPHY

The Coquette; or, The History of Eliza Wharton (1797) was an immediate success. It was reprinted in 1802 by Ebenezer Larkin of Boston, the novel's original publisher, and on January 29, 1803 the *Boston Weekly Magazine* noted its remarkable sales. Only a few copies of the early editions of *The Coquette* have survived to the present since single copies of the book were often shared among a large circle of friends and neighbors who read and reread until the books quite literally fell apart. The novel enjoyed its greatest popularity between 1824 and 1828, when it was reprinted eight times. New editions appeared regularly until the last quarter of the nineteenth century, and it has been reprinted twice in the twentieth, by Herbert Ross Brown in a Facsimile Text Society edition (1939) and by William S. Osborne, in 1970, in a paperback edition bound with William Hill Brown's *The Power of Sympathy*.

BIOGRAPHY AND CRITICISM

Almost universally regarded as the best of the early American novels, Hannah Webster Foster's novel has often received a page or two of notice in the standard literary histories of America. For an annotated bibliography of secondary sources, see the entry on Foster in Patricia L. Parker's *Early American Fiction: A Reference Guide* (1984). Jane E. Locke, in "Historical Preface, Including a Memoir of the Author," published as an introduction to the 1855 edition of *The Coquette*, was one of the first critics to provide an extensive historical background for the novel, an account supplemented (and often contradicted) by novelist Caroline Dall's sensational *The Romance of the Association; or, One Last Glimpse of Charlotte Temple and Eliza Wharton* (1875), by Mary C. Crawford's *Romance of Old New England Churches* (1904), and by Charles K. Bolton's *The Elizabeth Whitman Mystery* (1912). For a more recent (and moderate) account, see also James Woodress, *A Yankee's Odyssey: The Life of Joel Barlow* (1958).

Although scant, some further information about Foster's biography

can be found in the standard sources, such as the *Dictionary of American Biography* (1931), *Notable American Women* (1971), *American Women Writers: A Reference Guide* (1980), and *The Dictionary of Literary Biography: Volume 37, American Writers of the Early Republic* (1985). See also, Frederick C. Pierce, *The Foster Genealogy* (1889); Robert L. Shurter, "Mrs. Hannah Webster Foster and the Early American Novel," *American Literature*, 4 (1932); M. R. and W. H. Webster, *The History and Genealogy of the Governor John Webster Family of Connecticut* (1915); and John P. C. Winship, *Historical Brighton* (1899).

Critical assessments of the novel can be found in Herbert Ross Brown, *The Sentimental Novel in America, 1889–1860* (1940); Cathy N. Davidson, "Flirting with Destiny: Ambivalence and Form in the Early American Sentimental Novel," *Studies in American Fiction*, 10 (1982); Davidson, *Revolution and the Word: The Rise of the Novel in America* (1986); Lillie Deming Loshe, *The Early American Novel, 1789–1830* (1907); Tremaine McDowell, "Sensibility in the Eighteenth-Century American Novel," *Studies in Philology*, 24 (1927); Henri Petter, *The Early American Novel* (1971); Frank Shuffleton, "Mrs. Foster's *Coquette* and the Decline of Brotherly Watch," *Studies in Eighteenth-Century Culture*, 16 (1986); and Walter P. Wenska, Jr., "*The Coquette* and the American Dream of Freedom," *Early American Literature*, 12 (1977–78), 243–55.

CHRONOLOGY OF
HANNAH WEBSTER FOSTER

1758 Born in Salisbury, Massachusetts, to Grant Webster, a merchant, and Hannah Wainwright Webster

1762 Sent to boarding school after death of her mother

1771 Moves to Boston

178(?) Begins publishing political pieces in Boston newspapers

1785 Marries the Reverend John Foster, four years her junior; moves to Brighton, Massachusetts, where John served as minister of the First Church

1786 Birth of first child (name unrecorded; probably died soon after birth)

1789 Birth of John Foster

1790 Birth of Hannah Foster

1793 Birth of Henry Foster

1794 Birth of Elizabeth (Eliza) Foster, who later, under her married name Eliza Lanesford Cushing, wrote novels such as *Saratoga; A Tale of the Revolution* (1824) and *Yorktown; An Historical Romance* (1826), and co-edited a Montreal monthly magazine, *The Literary Garland*

1796 Birth of Harriet Foster, who later, under her married name Harriet Vaughan Cheney, wrote such popular books as *A Peep at the Pilgrims in 1636* (1824) and *The Rivals of Acadia* (1827)

1797 *The Coquette; or, The History of Eliza Wharton; A Novel; Founded on Fact* (By a Lady of Massachusetts)

1798 *The Boarding School; or, Lessons of a Preceptress to Her Pupils*, a didactic novel

1802 Second edition of *The Coquette*; dramatization of the novel by J. Horatio Nichols as *The New England Coquette*

1804 Begins contributing anonymous pieces to *The Monthly Anthology or Magazine of Polite Literature*, later known as the *North American Review*

1840 Death of Hannah Webster Foster in Montreal at the home of her daughter, Eliza Lanesford Cushing

THE COQUETTE;
or, The History of Eliza Wharton

THE

COQUETTE;

OR, THE

HISTORY OF ELIZA WHARTON;

A

NOVEL;

FOUNDED ON FACT.

By a LADY of MASSACHUSETTS.

[Hannah Foster.]

Boston :

PRINTED BY SAMUEL ETHERIDGE,
FOR E. LARKIN,
No. 47, CORNHILL.

1797.

Letter I.

TO MISS LUCY FREEMAN.

NEW-HAVEN.

A N unusual sensation possesses my breast; a sensation, which I once thought could never pervade it on any occasion whatever. It is *pleasure*; pleasure, my dear Lucy, on leaving my paternal roof! Could you have believed that the darling child of an indulgent and dearly beloved mother would feel a gleam of joy at leaving her? but so it is. The melancholy, the gloom, the condolence, which surrounded me for a month after the death of Mr. Haly, had depressed my spirits, and palled every enjoyment of life. Mr. Haly was a man of worth; a man of real and substantial merit. He is therefore deeply, and justly regreted by *his* friends; he was chosen to be a future guardian, and companion for me, and was, therefore, beloved by *mine*. As their choice; as a good man, and a faithful friend, I esteemed him. But no one acquainted with the disparity of our tempers and dispositions, our views and designs, can suppose my heart much engaged in the alliance. Both nature and education had instilled into my mind an implicit obedience to the will and desires of my parents. To them, of course, I sacrificed my fancy in this affair; determined that my reason should concur with theirs; and on that to risk my future happiness. I was the more encouraged, as I saw, from our first acquaintance, his declining health; and expected, that the event would prove as it has. Think not, however, that I rejoice in his death. No; far be it from me; for though I believe that I never felt the passion of love for Mr. Haly; yet a habit of conversing with him, of hearing daily the most virtuous, tender, and affec-

tionate sentiments from his lips, inspired emotions of the sincer-
est friendship, and esteem.

He is gone. His fate is unalterably, and I trust, happily fixed.
He lived the life, and died the death of the righteous. O that my
last end may be like his! This event will, I hope, make a suitable
and abiding impression upon my mind; teach me the fading na-
ture of all sublunary enjoyments, and the little dependence
which is to be placed on earthly felicity. Whose situation was
more agreeable; whose prospects more flattering, than Mr.
Haly's? Social, domestic, and connubial joys were fondly antici-
pated, and friends, and fortune seemed ready to crown every
wish! Yet animated by still brighter hopes, he cheerfully bid
them all adieu. In conversation with me, but a few days before
his exit; "There is" said he, "but one link in the chain of life,
undissevered; that, my dear Eliza, is my attachment to you. But
God is wise and good in all his ways; and in this, as in all other
respects, I would cheerfully say, His will be done."

You, my friend, were witness to the concluding scene; and
therefore, I need not describe it.

I shall only add, on the subject, that if I have wisdom and pru-
dence to follow his advice and example; if his prayers for my tem-
poral and eternal welfare be heard and answered, I shall be
happy indeed.

The disposition of mind, which I now feel, I wish to cultivate.
Calm, placid, and serene; thoughtful of my duty, and benevo-
lent to all around me, I wish for no other connection than that of
friendship,

This Letter is all egotism, I have even neglected to mention the
respectable, and happy friends, with whom I reside; but will do
it in my next. Write soon, and often; and believe me sincerely
yours,

ELIZA WHARTON.

LETTER II.

TO THE SAME

NEW-HAVEN.

TIME, which effaces every occasional impression, I find gradually dispelling the pleasing pensiveness, which the melancholy event, the subject of my last, had diffused over my mind. Naturally cheerful, volatile, and unreflecting, the opposite disposition, I have found to contain sources of enjoyment, which I was before unconscious of possessing.

My friends, here, are the picture of conjugal felicity. The situation is delightful. The visiting parties perfectly agreeable. Every thing tends to facilitate the return of my accustomed vivacity. I have written to my mother, and received an answer. She praises my fortitude, and admires the philosophy which I have exerted, under, what she calls, my heavy bereavement. Poor woman! She little thinks that my heart was untouched; and when that is unaffected, other sentiments and passions make but a transient impression. I have been, for a month or two, excluded from the gay world; and, indeed, fancied myself soaring above it. It is now that I begin to descend, and find my natural propensity for mixing in the busy scenes and active pleasures of life returning. I have received your letter; your moral lecture rather; and be assured, my dear, your monitorial lessons and advice shall be attended to. I believe I shall never again resume those airs, which you term *coquettish*, but which I think deserve a softer appellation; as they proceed from an innocent heart, and are the effusions of a youthful, and cheerful mind. We are all envited to spend the day, to morrow, at Col. Farington's, who has an elegant seat in this neighbourhood. Both he and his Lady are strangers to me; but the friends, by whom I am introduced, will procure me a welcome reception. Adieu.

ELIZA WHARTON.

Letter III.

TO THE SAME.

NEW-HAVEN.

I S it time for me to talk again of conquests? or must I only enjoy them in silence? I must write to you the impulses of my mind; or I must not write at all. You are not so morose, as to wish me to become a nun, would our country, and religion allow it. I ventured yesterday to throw aside the habiliments of mourning, and to array myself in those more adapted to my taste. We arrived at Col. Farington's about one o'clock. The Col. handed me out of the carriage, and introduced me to a large company assembled in the Hall. My name was pronounced with an *emphasis;* and I was received with the most flattering tokens of respect. When we were summoned to dinner, a young gentleman in a clerical dress offered me his hand, and led me to a table furnished with an elegant, and sumptuous repast, with more gallantry, and address than commonly fall to the share of students. He sat opposite me at table; and whenever I raised my eye, it caught his. The ease, and politeness of his manners, with his particular attention to me, raised my curiosity, and induced me to ask Mrs. Laiton who he was? She told me that his name was Boyer; that he was descended from a worthy family; had passed with honor and applause through the university where he was educated; had since studied divinity with success; and now had a call to settle as a minister in one of the first parishes in a neighbouring state.

The gates of a spacious garden were thrown open, at this instant; and I accepted with avidity an invitation to walk in it. Mirth, and hilarity prevailed, and the moments fled on downy wings; while we traced the beauties of art and nature, so liberally displayed, and so happily blended in this delightful retreat. An

enthusiastic admirer of scenes like these, I had rambled some way from the company, when I was followed by Mrs. Laiton to offer her condolence on the supposed loss, which I had sustained, in the death of Mr. Haly. My heart rose against the woman, so ignorant of human nature, as to think such conversation acceptable at such a time. I made her little reply, and waved the subject, though I could not immediately dispel the gloom which it excited.

The absurdity of a custom, authorising people at a first interview to revive the idea of griefs, which time has lulled, perhaps obliterated, is intolerable. To have our enjoyments arrested by the empty compliments of unthinking persons, for no other reason, than a compliance with fashion is to be treated in a manner, which the laws of humanity forbid.

We were soon joined by the gentlemen, who each selected his partner, and the walk was prolonged.

Mr. Boyer offered me his arm, which I gladly accepted; happy to be relieved from the impertinence of my female companion. We returned to tea, after which the ladies sung, and played by turns on the Piano Forte; while some of the gentlemen accompanied with the flute, the clarinet, and the violin, forming in the whole a very decent concert. An elegant supper, and half an hour's conversation after it, closed the evening; when we returned home, delighted with our entertainment and pleased with ourselves and each other. My imagination is so impressed with the festive scenes of the day, that Morpheus waves his ebon-wand in vain. The evening is fine beyond the power of description! all nature is serene and harmonious; in perfect unison with my present disposition of mind. I have been taking a retrospect of my past life; and a few juvenile follies excepted, which I trust the recording angel has blotted out with the tear of charity, find an approving conscience, and a heart at ease. Fortune, indeed, has not been very liberal of her gifts to me; but I presume on a large stock in the bank of friendship, which, united with health and innocence, give me some pleasing anticipations of future felicity.

Whatever my fate may be, I shall always continue your

ELIZA WHARTON.

LETTER IV.

TO MR. SELBY.

NEW-HAVEN.

YOU ask me, my friend, whether I am in pursuit of truth, or a lady? I answer, both. I hope and trust they are united; and really expect to find truth and the virtues and graces besides in a fair form. If you mean by the first part of your question, whether I am searching into the sublimer doctrines of religion? To these I would by no means be inattentive; but to be honest, my studies of that kind have been very much interrupted of late. The respectable circle of acquaintances with which I am honored here, has rendered my visits very frequent and numerous. In one of these I was introduced to Miss Eliza Wharton; a young lady whose elegant person, accomplished mind, and polished manners have been much celebrated. Her fame has often reached me; but, as the queen of Sheba said to Solomon, the half was not told me. You will think, that I talk in the style of a lover. I confess it, nor am I ashamed to rank myself among the professed admirers of this lovely fair one. I am in no danger, however, of becoming an enthusiastic devotee. No, I mean to act upon just and rational principles. Expecting soon to settle in an eligible situation, if such a companion as I am persuaded she will make me, may fall to my lot, I shall deem myself as happy as this state of imperfection will admit. She is now resident at Gen. Richman's. The general and his lady are her particular friends. They are warm in her praises. They tell me, however, that she is naturally of a gay disposition. No matter for that; it is an agreeable quality, where there is discretion sufficient for its regulation. A cheerful

friend, much more a cheerful wife is peculiarly necessary to a person of a studious and sedentary life. They dispel the gloom of retirement, and exhilerate the spirits depressed by intense application. She was formerly addressed by the late Mr. Haly of Boston. He was not, it seems, the man of her choice; but her parents were extremely partial to him, and wished the connection to take place. She, like a dutiful child, sacrificed her own inclination to their pleasure, so far as to acquiesce in his visits. This she more easily accomplished, as his health, which declined from their first acquaintance, led her to suppose, as the event has proved, that he would not live to enter into any lasting engagements. Her father, who died some months before him, invited him to reside at his house, for the benefit of a change of air, agreeably to the advice of his physicians. She attended him during his last illness, with all the care and assiduity of a nurse; and with all the sympathising tenderness of a sister.

I have had several opportunities of conversing with her. She discovers an elevated mind, a ready apprehension, and an accurate knowledge of the various subjects which have been brought into view. I have not yet introduced the favorite subject of my heart. Indeed she seems studiously to avoid noticing any expression which leads towards it. But she must hear it soon. I am sure of the favor and interest of the friends with whom she resides. They have promised to speak previously in my behalf. I am to call as if accidentally this afternoon, just as they are to ride abroad. They are to refer me to Miss Wharton for entertainment, till their return. What a delightful opportunity for my purpose! I am counting the hours, nay, the very moments. Adieu. You shall soon hear again from your most obedient,

<div style="text-align: right">J. Boyer.</div>

LETTER V.

TO MISS LUCY FREEMAN.

NEW-HAVEN.

THESE bewitching charms of mine have a tendency to keep
my mind in a state of perturbation. I am so pestered with
these admirers; not that I am so very handsome neither; but I
don't know how it is, I am certainly very much the taste of the
other sex. Followed, flattered, and caressed; I have cards and
compliments in profusion. But I must try to be serious; for I
have, alas! one serious lover. As I promised you to be particular
in my writing, I suppose I must proceed methodically. Yester-
day we had a party to dine. Mr. Boyer was of the number. His at-
tention was immediately engrossed; and I soon perceived that
every word, every action, and every look was studied to gain my
approbation. As he sat next me at dinner, his assiduity and po-
liteness were pleasing; and as we walked together afterwards,
his conversation was improving. Mine was sentimental and se-
date; perfectly adapted to the taste of my gallant. Nothing, how-
ever, was said particularly expressive of his apparent wishes. I
studiously avoided every kind of discourse which might lead to
this topic. I wish not for a declaration from any one, especially
from one whom I could not repulse and do not intend to encour-
age at present. His conversation, so similar to what I had often
heard from a similar character, brought a deceased friend to
mind, and rendered me somewhat pensive. I retired directly af-
ter supper. Mr. Boyer had just taken leave.

Mrs. Richman came into my chamber as she was passing to
her own. Excuse my intrusion, Eliza, said she; I thought I would
just step in and ask you if you have passed a pleasant day?

Perfectly so, madam; and I have now retired to protract the en-
joyment by recollection. What, my dear, is your opinion of our

favorite Mr. Boyer? Declaring him your favorite, madam, is suffi-
cient to render me partial to him. But to be frank, independent of
that, I think him an agreeable man. Your heart, I presume, is
now free? Yes, and I hope it will long remain so. Your friends,
my dear, solicitous for your welfare, wish to see you suitably
and agreeably connected. I hope my friends will never again in-
terpose in my concerns of that nature. You, madam, who have
ever known my heart, are sensible, that had the Almighty
spared life, in a certain instance, I must have sacrificed my own
happiness, or incurred their censure. I am young, gay, volatile.
A melancholy event has lately extricated me from those shack-
les, which parental authority had imposed on my mind. Let me
then enjoy that freedom which I so highly prize. Let me have op-
portunity, unbiassed by opinion, to gratify my natural disposi-
tion in a participation of those pleasures which youth and inno-
cence afford. Of such pleasures, no one, my dear, would wish to
deprive you. But beware, Eliza!—Though strowed* with flow-
ers, when contemplated by your lively imagination, it is, after
all, a slippery, thorny path. The round of fashionable dissipation
is dangerous. A phantom is often pursued, which leaves its de-
luded votary the real form of wretchedness. She spoke with an
emphasis, and taking up her candle, wished me a good night. I
had not power to return the compliment. Something seemingly
prophetic in her looks and expressions, cast a momentary gloom
upon my mind! But I despise those contracted ideas which con-
fine virtue to a cell. I have no notion of becoming a recluse. Mrs.
Richman has ever been a beloved friend of mine; yet I always
thought her rather prudish. Adieu,

ELIZA WHARTON.

*Strewn—ed.

LETTER VI.

TO THE SAME.

NEW-HAVEN.

I HAD scarcely seated myself at the breakfast table this morn-
ing, when a servant entered with a card of invitation from Ma-
jor Sanford, requesting the happiness of my hand this evening,
at a ball, given by Mr. Atkins, about three miles from this. I
shewed the billet to Mrs. Richman, saying, I have not much ac-
quaintance with this gentleman, madam; but I suppose his char-
acter sufficiently respectable to warrant an affirmative answer.
He is a gay man, my dear, to say no more, and such are the com-
panions we wish, when we join a party avowedly formed for
pleasure. I then stepped into my apartment, wrote an answer,
and dispatched the servant. When I returned to the parlour,
something disapprobating appeared in the countenances of both
my friends. I endeavored without seeming to observe, to dissi-
pate it by chit chat; but they were better pleased with each other
than with me; and soon rising, walked into the garden, and left
me to amuse myself alone. My eyes followed them through the
window. Happy pair, said I. Should it ever be my fate to wear
the hymenial chain, may I be thus united! The purest and most
ardent affection, the greatest consonance of taste and disposi-
tion, and the most congenial virtue and wishes distinguish this
lovely couple. Health and wealth, with every attendant blessing
preside over their favored dwelling, and shed their benign influ-
ence without alloy. The consciousness of exciting their displea-
sure gave me pain; but I consoled myself with the idea that it
was ill founded.

They should consider, said I, that they have no satisfaction to
look for beyond each other.

There every enjoyment is centered; but I am a poor solitary being, who need some amusement beyond what I can supply myself. The mind, after being confined at home for a while, sends the imagination abroad in quest of new treasures, and the body may as well accompany it, for ought I can see.

General Richman and lady have ever appeared solicitous to promote my happiness since I have resided with them. They have urged my acceptance of invitations to join parties, though they have not been much themselves, of late; as Mrs. Richman's present circumstances render her fond of retirement. What reason can be assigned for their apparent reluctance to this evening's entertainment is to me incomprehensible; but I shall apply the chymical powers of friendship and extract the secret from Mrs. Richman to morrow, if not before. Adieu. I am now summoned to dinner, and after that shall be engaged in preparation till the wished for hour of hilarity and mirth engrosses every faculty of your

<div align="right">ELIZA WHARTON.</div>

LETTER VII.

TO MR. SELBY.

<div align="right">NEW-HAVEN.</div>

DIVINES need not declaim, nor philosophers expatiate on the disappointments of human life! Are they not legibly written on every page of our existence? Are they not predominantly prevalent over every period of our lives?

When I closed my last letter to you, my heart exulted in the pleasing anticipation of promised bliss; my wishes danced on the light breezes of hope, and my imagination dared to arrest the

attention, and even claim a return of affection from the lovely Eliza Wharton! But imagination only, it has proved; and that dashed with the bitter ranklings of jealousy and suspicion.

But to resume my narrative. I reached the mansion of my friend about four. I was disagreeably struck with the appearance of a carriage at the door, as it raised an idea of company which might frustrate my plan; but still more disagreeable were my sensations, when, on entering the parlour, I found Major Sanford evidently in a waiting posture. I was very politely received; and when Eliza entered the room with a brilliance of appearance and gaiety of manner, which I had never before connected with her character, I rose, as did Major Sanford who offered his hand, and led her to a chair. I forgot to sit down again, but stood transfixed by the pangs of disappointment. Miss Wharton appeared somewhat confused; but soon resuming her vivacity, desired me to be seated; inquired after my health, and made some common place remarks on the weather. Then apologizing for leaving me, gave her hand again to Major Sanford, who had previously risen, and reminded her that the time and their engagements made it necessary to leave the good company; which, indeed, they both appeared very willing to do. General Richman and lady took every method in their power to remove my chagrin, and atone for the absence of my fair one, but ill did they succeed. They told me that Miss Wharton had not the most distant idea of my visiting there, this afternoon; much less of the design of my visit; that for some months together, she had been lately confined by the sickness of Mr. Haly, whom she attended during the whole of his last illness; which confinement had eventually increased her desire of indulging her natural disposition for gaiety. She had, however, they said, an excellent heart and reflecting mind, a great share of sensibility, and a temper peculiarly formed for the enjoyments of social life. But this gentleman, madam, who is her gallant this evening—is his character unexceptionable? Will a lady of delicacy associate with an immoral, not to say profligate man? The rank and fortune of Major Sanford, said Mrs. Richman, procure him respect.

His specious manners render him acceptable in public company; but I must own that he is not the person with whom I wish my cousin to be connected, even for a moment. She never consulted me so little on any subject as on that of his card this morning. Before I had time to object, she dismissed the servant; and I forbore to destroy her expected happiness, by acquainting her with my disapprobation of her partner. Her omission was not design; it was juvenile indiscretion. We must, my dear sir, continued she, look with a candid eye on such excentricities. Faults, not foibles, require the severity of censure. Far, madam, be it from me to censure any conduct, which as yet I have observed in Miss Wharton; she has too great an interest in my heart to admit of that.

We now went into more general conversation. Tea was served; and I soon after took leave. General Richman, however, insisted on my dining with him on Thursday, which I promised. And here I am again over head and ears in the hypo.* A disease, you will say, peculiar to students. I believe it peculiar to lovers; and with that class I must now rank myself, though I did not know, until this evening, that I was so much engaged as I find I really am. I knew, indeed, that I was extremely pleased with this amiable girl; that I was interested in her favor; that I was happier in her company than any where else, with innumerable other circumstances, which would have told me the truth, had I examined them. But be that as it may; I hope, and trust that I am, and ever shall be a reasonable creature; and not suffer my judgment to be misled by the operations of a blind passion.

I shall now lay aside this subject, endeavor to divest even my imagination of the charmer, and return until Thursday, to the contemplation of those truths and duties, which have a happy tendency to calm the jarring elements which compose our mortal frame. Adieu.

<div align="right">J. BOYER.</div>

*Melancholy; morbid depression of the spirits—ed.

LETTER VIII.

TO MR. CHARLES DEIGHTON.

NEW-HAVEN.

WE had an elegant ball, last night, Charles; and what is still
more to the taste of your old friend, I had an elegant part-
ner; one exactly calculated to please my fancy; gay, volatile, ap-
parently thoughtless of every thing but present enjoyment. It
was Miss Eliza Wharton, a young lady, whose agreeable person,
polished manners, and refined talents, have rendered her the
toast of the country around for these two years; though for half
that time she has had a clerical lover imposed on her by her
friends; for I am told it was not agreeable to her inclination. By
this same clerical lover of hers, she was for several months con-
fined as a nurse. But his death has happily relieved her, and she
now returns to the world with redoubled lustre. At present she
is a visitor to Mrs. Richman, who is a relation. I first saw her on a
party of pleasure at Mr. Frazier's where we walked, talked,
sung, and danced together. I thought her cousin watched her
with a jealous eye; for she is, you must know, a prude; and im-
maculate, more so than you or I must be the man who claims ad-
mission to her society. But I fancy this young lady is a coquette;
and if so, I shall avenge my sex, by retaliating the mischiefs, she
meditates against us. Not that I have any ill designs; but only to
play off her own artillery, by using a little unmeaning gallantry.
And let her beware of the consequences. A young clergyman
came in at Gen. Richman's yesterday, while I was waiting for
Eliza, who was much more cordially received by the general and
his lady, than was your humble servant: but I lay that up.

When she entered the room, an air of mutual embarrasment
was evident. The lady recovered her assurance much more eas-
ily than the gentleman. I am just going to ride, and shall make it

in my way to call and inquire after the health of my dulcinea. Therefore, adieu for the present.

PETER SANFORD.

LETTER IX.

TO MISS LUCY FREEMAN.

NEW-HAVEN.

I AM not so happy to day in the recollection of last evening's entertainment, as I was in the enjoyment.

The explanation which I promised you from Mrs. Richman yesterday, I could not obtain. When I went down to dinner, some friends of General Richman's had accidentally dropped in, which precluded all particular conversation. I retired soon to dress, and saw Mrs. Richman no more, till I was informed that Major Sanford waited for me. But I was surprised on going into the parlour to find Mr. Boyer there. I blushed and stammered; but I know not why; for certain I am, that I neither love nor fear the good man yet, whatever I may do some future day. I would not be understood that I do not respect and esteem him; for I do both. But these are calm passions, which sooth rather than agitate the mind. It was not the consciousness of any impropriety of conduct; for I was far from feeling any. The entertainment for which I was prepared was such as virtue would not disapprove, and my gallant was a man of fortune, fashion, and for ought I knew, of unblemished character.

But Mr. Boyer was much more disconcerted than myself. Indeed he did not recover his philosophy while I staid. I believe, by some hints I have received since, that he had some particular views, in which he was disappointed.

Our ball had every charm which could render a ball delightful.

My partner was all ease, politeness, and attention; and your friend was as much flattered and caressed as variety itself could wish. We returned to General Richman's about two. Major Sanford asked leave to call and inquire after my health, this morning, and I am now expecting him. I rose to breakfast. The late hour of retiring to rest had not depressed, but rather exhilerated my spirits. My friends were waiting for me in the parlor. They received me sociably, inquired after my health, my last evening's entertainment, the company, &c. When, after a little pause, Mrs. Richman said, and how do you like Major Sanford, Eliza? Very well indeed, madam: I think him a finished gentleman. Will you, who are a connoisieur, allow him that title? No, my dear: in my opinion, he falls far below it; since he is deficient in one of the great essentials of the character, and that is, *virtue*. I am surprised, said I: but how has he incurred so severe a censure? By being a professed libertine; by having but too successfully practised the arts of seduction; by triumphing in the destruction of innocence and the peace of families!

O, why was I not informed of this before? But, perhaps, these are old affairs; the effects of juvenile folly; crimes of which he may have repented, and which charity ought to obliterate. No, my dear, they are recent facts; facts which he dares not deny; facts for which he ought to be banished from all virtuous society. I should have intimated this to you before, but your precipitate acceptance of his invitation deprived me of an opportunity, until it was too late to prevent your going with him; and we thought it best to protract your enjoyment as long as possible, not doubting but your virtue and delicacy would, in future, guard you against the like deception.

Must I then become an avowed prude at once; and refuse him admission, if he call, in compliance with the customary forms? By no means. I am sensible, that even the false maxims of the world must be complied with in a degree. But a man of Major Sanford's art can easily distinguish between a forbidding, and an encouraging reception. The former may, in this case, be given without any breach of the rules of politeness. Astonished, and

mortified, I knew not what further to say. I had been so pleased with the man, that I wished to plead in his favor; but virtue and prudence forbade. I therefore rose and retired. He is this moment, I am told, below stairs. So that I must bid you adieu, until the next post.

ELIZA WHARTON.

LETTER X.

TO THE SAME.

NEW-HAVEN.

UPON closing my last, I walked down, and found Major Sanford alone. He met me at the door of the parlor; and taking my hand with an air of affectionate tenderness, led me to a seat, and took one beside me. I believe the gloom of suspicion had not entirely forsaken my brow. He appeared, however, not to notice it; but after the compliments of the day had passed, entered into an easy and agreeable conversation on the pleasures of society: a conversation perfectly adapted to my taste, and calculated to dissipate my chagrin, and pass the time imperceptibly. He inquired the place of my native abode; and having informed him, he said he had thoughts of purchasing the seat of Capt. Pribble, in that neighborhood, for his residence; and could he be assured of my society and friendship, his resolution would be fixed. I answered his compliment only by a slight bow. He took leave, and I retired to dress for the day, being engaged to accompany my cousin to dine at Mr. Laurence's, a gentleman of fortune and fashion, in this vicinity. Mr. Laurence has but one daughter, heiress to a large estate, with an agreeable form, but a countenance, which to me, indicates not much soul. I was surprised in the afternoon to see Major Sanford alight at the gate. He entered with

the familiarity of an old acquaintance; and, after accosting each
of the company, told me, with a low bow, that he did not expect
the happiness of seeing me again so soon. I received his compli-
ment with a conscious awkwardness. Mrs. Richman's morning
lecture still rung in my head; and her watchful eye now traced ev-
ery turn of mine, and every action of the major's. Indeed, his as-
siduity was painful to me; yet I found it impossible to disengage
myself a moment from him, till the close of the day brought our
carriage to the door; when he handed me in, and pressing my
hand to his lips, retired.

What shall I say about this extraordinary man? Shall I own to
you, my friend, that he is pleasing to me? His person, his man-
ners, his situation, all combine to charm my fancy; and to my
lively imagination, strew the path of life with flowers. What a
pity, my dear Lucy, that the graces and virtues are not oftner
united! They must, however, meet in the man of my choice; and
till I find such a one, I shall continue to subscribe my name

<div align="right">Eliza Wharton.</div>

Letter XI.

TO MR. CHARLES DEIGHTON.

<div align="right">NEW-HAVEN.</div>

WELL, Charles, I have been manœuvring to day, a little re-
vengefully. That, you will say, is out of character. So bale-
ful a passion does not easily find admission among those softer
ones, which you well know I cherish. However, I am a mere Pro-
teus, and can assume any shape that will best answer my pur-
pose.

I called this forenoon, as I told you I intended, at Gen.
Richman's. I waited some time in the parlor alone, before Eliza

appeared; and when she did appear, the distant reserve of her manners and the pensiveness of her countenance convinced me that she had been vexed, and I doubted not but Peter Sanford was the occasion. Her wise cousin, I could have sworn, had been giving her a detail of the vices of her gallant; and warning her against the danger of associating with him in future. Notwithstanding, I took no notice of any alteration in her behavior; but entered with the utmost facetiousness into a conversation which I thought most to her taste. By degrees, she assumed her usual vivacity; cheerfulness and good humor again animated her countenance. I tarried as long as decency would admit. She having intimated that they were to dine at my friend Lawrence's, I caught at this information; and determined to follow them, and teaze the jealous Mrs. Richman, by playing off all the gallantry I was master of in her presence.

I went, and succeeded to the utmost of my wishes, as I read in the vexation, visible in the one; and the ease and attention displayed by the other. I believe too, that I have charmed the eye at least, of the amiable Eliza. Indeed, Charles, she is a fine girl. I think it would hurt my conscience to wound her mind or reputation. Were I disposed to marry, I am persuaded she would make an excellent wife; but that you know is no part of my plan, so long as I can keep out of the noose. Whenever I do submit to be shackled, it must be from a necessity of mending my fortune. This girl would be far from doing that. However, I am pleased with her acquaintance, and mean not to abuse her credulity and good nature, if I can help it.

PETER SANFORD.

LETTER XII.

TO MISS LUCY FREEMAN.

NEW-HAVEN.

THE heart of your friend is again besieged. Whether it will surrender to the assailants or not, I am unable at present to determine. Sometimes I think of becoming a predestinarian, and submitting implicitly to fate, without any exercise of free will; but, as mine seems to be a wayward one, I would counteract the operations of it, if possible.

Mrs. Richman told me this morning, that she hoped I should be as agreeably entertained this afternoon, as I had been the preceding; that she expected Mr. Boyer to dine, and take tea; and doubted not but he would be as attentive and sincere to me, if not as gay and polite as the gentleman who obtruded his civilities yesterday. I replied that I had no reason to doubt the sincerity of the one, or the other, having never put them to the test, nor did I imagine I ever should. Your friends, Eliza, said she, would be very happy to see you united to a man of Mr. Boyer's worth; and so agreeably settled, as he has a prospect of being. I hope, said I, that my friends are not so weary of my company, as to wish to dispose of me. I am too happy in my present connections to quit them for new ones. Marriage is the tomb of friendship. It appears to me a very selfish state. Why do people, in general, as soon as they are married, centre all their cares, their concerns, and pleasures in their own families? former acquaintances are neglected or forgotten. The tenderest ties between friends are weakened, or dissolved; and benevolence itself moves in a very limited sphere. It is the glory of the marriage state, she rejoined, to refine, by circumscribing our enjoyments. Here we can repose in safety.

"The friendships of the world are oft
Confed'racies in vice, or leagues in pleasure:
Our's has the purest virtue for its basis;
And such a friendship ends not but with life."

True, we cannot always pay that attention to former associates, which we may wish; but the little community which we superintend is quite as important an object; and certainly renders us more beneficial to the public. True benevolence, though it may change its objects, is not limited by time or place. Its effects are the same, and aided by a second self, are rendered more diffusive and salutary.

Some pleasantry passed, and we retired to dress. When summoned to dinner, I found Mr. Boyer below. If what is sometimes said be true, that love is diffident, reserved, and unassuming, this man must be tinctured with it. These symptoms were visible in his deportment when I entered the room. However, he soon recovered himself, and the conversation took a general turn. The festive board was crowned with sociability, and we found in reality, "The feast of reason, and the flow of soul." After we rose from table, a walk in the garden was proposed, an amusement we are all peculiarly fond of. Mr. Boyer offered me his arm. When at a sufficient distance from our company, he begged leave to congratulate himself on having an opportunity which he had ardently desired for some time, of declaring to me his attachment; and of soliciting an interest in my favor; or, if he might be allowed the term, affection. I replied, that, Sir, is indeed laying claim to an important interest. I believe you must substitute some more indifferent epithet for the present. Well then, said he, if it must be so, let it be esteem, or friendship. Indeed, Sir, said I, you are intitled to them both. Merit has always a share in that bank; and I know of none, who has a larger claim on that score, than Mr. Boyer. I suppose my manner was hardly serious enough for what he considered a weighty cause. He was a little disconcerted; but soon regaining his presence of mind, entreated me, with an air of earnestness, to encourage his suit, to

admit his addresses, and, if possible, to reward his love. I told him, that this was rather a sudden affair to me; and that I could not answer him without consideration. Well then, said he, take what time you think proper, only relieve my suspense as soon as may be. Shall I visit you again to morrow? O, not so soon, said I. Next Monday, I believe will be early enough. I will endeavor to be at home. He thanked me even for that favor, recommended himself once more to my kindness; and we walked towards the company, returned with them to the house, and he soon took leave. I immediately retired to write this letter, which I shall close, without a single observation on the subject, until I know your opinion.

<div align="right">ELIZA WHARTON.</div>

LETTER XIII.

TO MISS ELIZA WHARTON.

<div align="right">HARTFORD.</div>

AND so you wish to have my opinion before you know the result of your own. This is playing a little too much with my patience. But, however, I will gratify you this once, in hopes that my epistle may have a good effect. You will ask, perhaps, whether I would influence your judgment? I answer, no; provided you will exercise it yourself: but I am a little apprehensive that your fancy will mislead you. Methinks I can gather from your letters, a predilection for this Major Sanford. But he is a rake, my dear friend; and can a lady of your delicacy and refinement, think of forming a connection with a man of that character? I hope not. Nay, I am confident you do not. You mean only to exhibit a few more girlish airs, before you turn matron. But I am persuaded, if you wish to lead down the dance of life

with regularity, you will not find a more excellent partner than Mr. Boyer. Whatever you can reasonably expect in a lover, husband, or friend, you may perceive to be united in this worthy man. His taste is undebauched, his manners not vitiated, his morals uncorrupted. His situation in life is, perhaps, as elevated as you have a right to claim. Forgive my plainness, Eliza. It is the task of friendship, sometimes to tell disagreeable truths. I know your ambition is to make a distinguished figure in the first class of polished society; to shine in the gay circle of fashionable amusements, and to bear off the palm amidst the votaries of pleasure. But these are fading honors, unsatisfactory enjoyments; incapable of gratifying those immortal principles of reason and religion, which have been implanted in your mind by nature; assiduously cultivated by the best of parents, and exerted, I trust, by yourself. Let me advise you then, in conducting this affair; an affair, big, perhaps, with your future fate, to lay aside those coquettish airs which you sometimes put on; and remember that you are not dealing with a fop, who will take advantage of every concession; but with a man of sense and honor, who will properly estimate your condescension, and frankness. Act then with that modest freedom, that dignified unreserve which bespeaks conscious rectitude and sincerity of heart.

I shall be extremely anxious to hear the process and progress of this business. Relieve my impatience, as soon as possible, and believe me yours, with undissembled affection.

<div style="text-align: right">Lucy Freeman.</div>

LETTER XIV.

TO MISS LUCY FREEMAN.

NEW-HAVEN.

I HAVE received, and read again and again, your friendly epis-
tle. My reason and judgment entirely coincide with your opin-
ion; but my fancy claims some share in the decision: and I cannot
yet tell which will preponderate. This was the day fixed for decid-
ing Mr. Boyer's cause. My friends here gave me a long disserta-
tion on his merits. Your letter, likewise, had its weight, and I
was candidly summing up the *pros* and *cons* in the garden,
whither I had walked (Gen. Richman and lady having rode out)
when I was informed that he was waiting in the parlor. I went
immediately in (a good symptom, you will say) and received
him very graciously. After the first compliments were over, he
seemed eager to improve the opportunity to enter directly on the
subject of his present visit. It is needless for me to recite to you,
who have long been acquainted with the whole process of court-
ship, the declarations, propositions, protestations, intreaties,
looks, words and actions of a lover. They are, I believe, much
the same, in the whole sex, allowing for their different disposi-
tions, educations, and characters. But you are impatient I know
for the conclusion. You have hastily perused the preceding
lines, and are straining your eye forward to my part of the farce;
for such it may prove after all. Well then, not to play too long
with the curiosity, which I know to be excited, and actuated by
real friendship, I will relieve it. I think you would have been
pleased to have seen my gravity, on this important occasion.
With all the candor and frankness which I was capable of assum-
ing, I thus answered his long harangue, to which I had listened,
without interrupting him. Self-knowledge, sir, that most impor-
tant of all sciences, I have yet to learn. Such have been my situa-

tions in life, and the natural volatility of my temper, that I have looked but little into my own heart, in regard to its future wishes and views. From a scene of constraint and confinement, ill suited to my years and inclination, I have just launched into society. My heart beats high in expectation of its fancied joys. My sanguine imagination paints, in alluring colors, the charms of youth and freedom, regulated by virtue and innocence. Of these, I wish to partake. While I own myself under obligations for the esteem which you are pleased to profess for me, and in return, acknowledge, that neither your person nor manners are disagreeable to me, I recoil at the thought of immediately forming a connection, which must confine me to the duties of domestic life, and make me dependent for happiness, perhaps too, for subsistence, upon a class of people, who will claim the right of scrutinising every part of my conduct; and by censuring those foibles, which I am conscious of not having prudence to avoid, may render me completely miserable. While, therefore, I receive your visits, and cultivate towards you sentiments of friendship and esteem, I would not have you consider me as confined to your society, or obligated to a future connection. Our short acquaintance renders it impossible for me to decide what the operations of my mind may hereafter be. You must either quit the subject, or leave me to the exercise of my free will, which perhaps may coincide with your present wishes. Madam, said he, far is the wish from me to restrain your person or mind. In your breast I will repose my cause. It shall be my study to merit a return of affection; and I doubt not, but generosity and honor will influence your conduct towards me. I expect soon to settle among a generous and enlightened people, where I flatter myself I shall be exempt from those difficulties, and embarrassments, to which too many of my brethren are subject. The local situation is agreeable, the society refined and polished; and if, in addition, I may obtain that felicity which you are formed to bestow, in a family connection, I shall be happy indeed.

He spoke with emphasis. The tear of sensibility sparkled in his eye. I involuntarily gave him my hand, which he pressed with ar-

dor to his lips. Then rising, he walked to the window to conceal his emotion. I rang the bell and ordered tea; during, and after which, we shared that social converse, which is the true zest of life, and which, I am persuaded, none but virtuous minds can participate. General Richman and lady returned with the shades of the evening. The penetrating eye of my cousin traced in *our* countenances the progress of the cause, and the smile of approbation animated *hers*. Mr. Boyer asked the favor of my company to ride to morrow morning, which was granted. He tarried to supper, and took his leave. I retired immediately to my chamber, to which I was followed by Mrs. Richman. I related to her the conversation, and the encouragement which I had given to Mr. Boyer. She was pleased; but insisted that I should own myself somewhat engaged to him. This, I told her I should never do to any man, before the indissoluble knot was tied. That, said I, will be time enough to resign my freedom. She replied that I had wrong ideas of freedom, and matrimony; but she hoped that Mr. Boyer would happily rectify them.

I have now, my dear friend, given you an account of my present situation, and leave you to judge for yourself concerning it. Write me your opinion, and believe me ever yours.

ELIZA WHARTON.

LETTER XV.

TO MISS ELIZA WHARTON.

HARTFORD.

I CONGRATULATE you, my dear Eliza, on the stability of your conduct towards Mr. Boyer. Pursue the system which you have adopted, and I dare say, that happiness will crown your future days. You are indeed very tenacious of your free-

dom, as you call it; but that is a play about words. A man of Mr.
Boyer's honor and good sense will never abridge any privileges
which virtue can claim.

When do you return to embellish our society, here? I am impa-
tient to see you, and likewise this amiable man. I am much inter-
ested in his favor. By the way, I am told that Major Sanford has
been to look at the seat of Captain Pribble, which is upon sale. It
is reported that he will probably purchase it. Many of our gentry
are pleased with the prospect of such a neighbor. As an accom-
plished gentleman, say they, he will be an agreeable addition to
our social parties; and as a man of property, and public spirit, he
will be an advantage to the town; but, from what I have heard of
him, I am far from supposing him a desirable acquisition in ei-
ther of these respects. A man of a vicious character cannot be a
good member of society. In order to that, his principles and prac-
tice must be uncorrupted: in his morals, at least, he must be a
man of probity, and honor. Of these qualifications, if I mistake
not, this gallant of yours cannot boast. But I shall not set up for a
censor. I hope neither you nor I shall have much connection
with him. My swain interests himself very much in your affairs.
You will possibly think him impertinent; but I give his curiosity a
softer name. Should I own to you that I place great confidence in
his integrity and honor, you would, perhaps, laugh at my weak-
ness; but, my dear, I have pride enough to keep me above
coquettry, or prudery; and discretion enough, I hope, to secure
me from the errors of both. With him I have determined to walk
the future round of life. What folly then would it be to affect re-
serve and distance, relative to an affair in which I have so much
interest? Not that I am going to betray your secrets. These I have
no right to divulge; but I must be the judge what may, and what
may not be communicated. I am very much pressed for an early
day of consummation; but I shall not listen to a request of that
kind, till your return. Such is my regard for you, that a union of
love would be imperfect, if friendship attended not the rites.
Adieu.

LUCY FREEMAN.

LETTER XVI.

TO MISS LUCY FREEMAN.

NEW-HAVEN.

WE go on charmingly here; almost as soft and smooth as your ladyship. It seems to me that love must stagnate, if it have not a light breeze of discord once in a while to keep it in motion. We have not tried any yet, however. We had a lovely tour this forenoon; were out three long hours, and returned to dinner in perfect harmony.

Mr. Boyer informed me that he should set out to morrow morning, for his future residence, and soon put on the sacred bands. He solicited an epistolary correspondence, at the same time, as an alleviation of the care which that weighty charge would bring on his mind. I consented; telling him, that he must not expect any thing more than general subjects from me.

We were somewhat interrupted in our confidential intercourse, in the afternoon, by the arrival of Major Sanford. I cannot say that I was not agreeably relieved. So sweet a repast, for several hours together, was rather sickening to my taste. My enamorato looked a little mortified at the cheerful reception which I gave the intruder, and joined not so placidly in the social conversation, as I could have wished.

When Mr. Boyer, after the Major took leave, pressed me to give him some assurance of my constancy, I only reminded him of the terms of our engagement. Seeing me decided, he was silent on the subject, and soon bid me an affectionate adieu; not expecting, as he told me, the pleasure of a personal interview again, for two or three months.

Thus far we have proceeded in this sober business. A good beginning, you will say. Perhaps it is. I do not, however, feel myself greatly interested in the progress of the negociation. Time

may consolidate my affections, and enable me to fix them on some particular object. At present the most lively emotions of my heart are those of friendship; that friendship which I hope you will soon participate with your faithful

<div align="right">ELIZA WHARTON.</div>

LETTER XVII.

TO MR. SELBY.

<div align="right">NEW-HAVEN.</div>

I HAVE succeeded in my addresses to the lovely Eliza Wharton; as far at least as I had any reason to expect from our short acquaintance. I find the graces of her person and mind rise in my esteem; and have already enjoyed, in her society, some of the happiest hours of my life. She is kind, affable, and condescending; yet I must own that I have not been able to infuse into her bosom, the ardor which I feel in my own. I know that the native modesty of the sex would restrain the discovery; but there is an animation of countenance, which betrays the sensations of the heart, that I find wanting in hers on this occasion.

I have just taken leave of my fair, and propose returning to morrow morning; to take upon me the solemn charge, which lies with such weight upon my mind, that I need every support, both human and divine. Eliza has promised to correspond with me. From this I anticipate a source of pleasure, which alone can atone for her absence. I am, &c.

<div align="right">J. BOYER.</div>

LETTER XVIII.

TO MR. CHARLES DEIGHTON.

NEW-HAVEN.

D O you know, Charles, that I have commenced lover? I was always a general one; but now I am somewhat particular. I shall be the more interested, as I am likely to meet with difficulties; and it is the glory of a rake, as well as a Christian to combat obstacles. This same Eliza, of whom I have told you, has really made more impression on my heart, than I was aware of; or than the sex, take them as they rise, are wont to do. But she is besieged by a priest (a likely lad though.) I know not how it is, but they are commonly successful with the girls, even the gayest of them. This one, too, has the interest of all her friends, as I am told. I called yesterday, at General Richman's, and found this pair together, apparently too happy in each other's society for my wishes. I must own, that I felt a glow of jealousy, which I never experienced before; and vowed revenge for the pain it gave me, though but momentary. Yet Eliza's reception of me was visibly cordial; nay, I fancied my company as pleasing to her as that which she had before. I tarried not long, but left him to the enjoyment of that pleasure which I flatter myself will be short-lived. O, I have another plan in my head; a plan of necessity, which, you know, is the mother of invention. It is this: I am very much courted and caressed by the family of Mr. Lawrence, a man of large property in this neighborhood. He has only one child; a daughter, with whom I imagine the old folks intend to shackle me in the bonds of matrimony. The girl looks very well. She has no soul though, that I can discover. She is heiress, nevertheless, to a great fortune; and that is all the soul I wish for in a wife. In truth, Charles, I know of no other way to mend my circumstances. But lisp not a word of my embarrassments for your

life. Show and equipage are my hobby-horse; and if any female wish to share them with me, and will furnish me with the means of supporting them, I have no objection. Could I conform to the sober rules of wedded life, and renounce those dear enjoyments of dissipation, in which I have so long indulged, I know not the lady in the world with whom I would sooner form a connection of this sort than with Eliza Wharton. But it will never do. If my fortune, or hers were better, I would risk a union; but as they are, no idea of the kind can be admitted. I shall endeavor, notwithstanding, to enjoy her company as long as possible. Though I cannot possess her wholly myself, I will not tamely see her the property of another.

I am now going to call at General Richman's, in hopes of an opportunity to profess my devotion to her. I know I am not a welcome visitor to the family; but I am independent of their censure or esteem, and mean to act accordingly.

PETER SANFORD.

LETTER XIX.

TO MISS LUCY FREEMAN.

NEW-HAVEN.

I FIND the ideas of sobriety, and domestic solitude, I have been cultivating for three days past, somewhat deranged by the interruption of a visitor, with whom, I know, you will not be pleased. It is no other than Major Sanford. I was walking alone in the garden yesterday, when he suddenly appeared to my view. How happy am I, said he, seizing my hand, in this opportunity of finding you alone; an opportunity, Miss Wharton, which I must improve in expatiating on a theme, that fills my heart, and solely animates my frame.

I was startled at his impetuosity, and displeased with his free-
dom. Withdrawing my hand, I told him, that my retirement was
sacred. He bowed submissively; begged pardon for his intru-
sion, alledged, that he found no body but the servants in the
house; that they informed him, I was alone in the garden, which
intelligence was too pleasing for him to consult any forms of cere-
mony for the regulation of his conduct. He then went on rhap-
sodically to declare his passion, his suspicions, that I was form-
ing a connection with Mr. Boyer, which would effectually de-
stroy all his hopes of future happiness. He painted the restraint,
the confinement, the embarrassments to which a woman, con-
nected with a man of Mr. Boyer's profession, must be subjected;
however agreeable his person might be. He asked if my gener-
ous mind could submit to cares and perplexities like these;
whether I could not find greater sources of enjoyment in a more
elevated sphere of life, or share pleasures better suited to my ge-
nius and disposition, even in a single state? I listened to him in-
voluntarily. My heart did not approve his sentiments, but my
ear was charmed with his rhetoric, and my fancy captivated by
his address.

He invited my confidence, by the most ardent professions of
friendship, and labored to remove my suspicions by vows of sin-
cerity. I was induced by his importunity, gradually to disclose
the state of affairs between Mr. Boyer and myself. He listened ea-
gerly; wished not, he said, to influence me unduly; but if I were
not otherwise engaged, might he presume to solicit a place in
my friendship and esteem; be admitted to enjoy my society, to
visit me as an acquaintance, and to attend my excursions and
amusements, as a brother, if no more? I replied, that I was a pen-
sioner of friendship, at present; that my friends were extremely
refined in their notions of propriety, and that I had no right to re-
ceive visitants independent of them. I understand you, madam,
said he. You intimate that my company is not agreeable to them:
but I know not why. Surely my rank in life is as elevated; and my
knowledge of, and acceptance in the world, are as extensive as
General Richman's. I hope, said I, since we are engaged in the

conversation, that you will excuse my frankness, if I tell you, that the understanding and virtue of this worthy couple, induce them, without any regard to rank, to bestow their esteem wherever it is merited. I cannot say that you are not a sharer. Your own heart can best determine, whether upon their principles, you are, or not! He appeared mortified, and chagrined; and we had walked some distance without exchanging a word, or a look. At last, he rejoined, I plead guilty to the charge, madam, which they have undoubtedly brought against me, of imprudence and folly in many particulars; yet of malignancy and vice I am innocent. Brought up in affluence; innured from my infancy to the gratification of every passion; the indulgence of every wish, it is not strange, that a life of dissipation and gaiety should prove alluring to a youthful mind, which had no care but to procure what it deemed enjoyment. In this pursuit I have perhaps deviated from the rigid rules of discretion, and the harsher laws of morality.

But let the veil of charity be drawn over my faults; let the eye of candor impartially examine my present behavior; let the kind and lenient hand of friendship assist in directing my future steps; and, perhaps, I may not prove unworthy of associating with the respectable inhabitants of this happy mansion; for such I am sure it must be, while honored with Miss Wharton's presence. But, circumstanced as you and I are, at present, I will not sue for your attention, as a lover; but rest contented, if possible, with that share of kindness, and regard, which your benevolence may afford me as a friend. I bowed in approbation of his resolution. He pressed my hand with ardor to his lips; and at that instant General Richman entered the garden. He approached us cheerfully, offered Major Sanford his hand with apparent cordiality, and told us pleasantly, that he hoped he should not be considered as an intruder. By no means, sir, said Major Sanford. It is I who have incurred that imputation. I called this afternoon to pay you my respects; when being informed that you and your lady were abroad, and that Miss Wharton was in the garden, I took the liberty to invade her retirement. She has

graciously forgiven my crime, and I was just affixing the seal to my pardon as you entered.

We then returned into the house. Mrs. Richman received us politely. During tea, the conversation turned on literary subjects, in which I cannot say that the Major bore a very distinguished part. After he was gone, Mrs. Richman said, I hope you have been agreeably entertained, Miss Wharton? I did not chuse* my company, madam, said I. Nor, said she, did you refuse it, I presume. Would you not have me respect the rights of hospitality towards your guests, when you are absent, madam? If you had acted from that motive, I own my obligations to you, my dear; but even that consideration can hardly reconcile me to the sacrifice of time, which you have made to the amusement of a seducer. I hope, madam, you do not think me an object of seduction! I do not think you seducible; nor was Richardson's Clarissa, till she made herself the victim, by her own indiscretion. Pardon me, Eliza, this is a second Lovelace. I am alarmed by his artful intrusions. His insinuating attention to you are characteristic of the man. Come, I presume you are not interested to keep his secrets, if you know them. Will you give me a little sketch of his conversation? Most willingly, said I; and, accordingly, related the whole. When I had concluded, she shook her head, and replied, beware, my friend, of his arts. Your own heart is too sincere to suspect treachery and dissimulation in another; but suffer not your ear to be charmed by the syren voice of flattery; nor your eye to be caught by the phantom of gaiety and pleasure. Remember your engagements to Mr. Boyer. Let sincerity and virtue be your guides, and they will lead you to happiness and peace. She waited not for an answer, but immediately rising, begged leave to retire, alledging that she was fatigued. Gen. Richman accompanied her, and I hastened to my apartment, where I have written thus far, and shall send it on for your comments. I begin to think of returning soon to your circle. One inducement is, that I may be free from the intrusions of this man. Adieu.

ELIZA WHARTON.

*Choose—ed.

LETTER XX.

TO MRS. M. WHARTON.

FROM the conversation of the polite, the sedate, the engaging and the gay; from corresponding with the learned, the sentimental and the refined, my heart and my pen turn with ardor and alacrity to a tender and affectionate parent, the faithful guardian and guide of my youth; the unchanging friend of my riper years. The different dispositions of various associates, sometimes perplex the mind, which seeks direction; but in the disinterested affection of the maternal breast, we fear no dissonance of passion, no jarring interests, no disunion of love. In this seat of felicity is every enjoyment which fancy can form, or friendship, with affluence, bestow; but still my mind frequently returns to the happy shades of my nativity. I wish there to impart my pleasures, and share the counsels of my best, my long tried and experienced friend. At this time, my dear mamma, I am peculiarly solicitous for your advice. I am again inportuned to listen to the voice of love; again called upon to accept the addresses of a gentleman of merit and respectability. You will know the character of the man, when I tell you, it is Mr. Boyer. But his situation in life! I dare not enter it. My disposition is not calculated for that sphere. There are duties arising from the station, which I fear I should not be able to fulfil; cares and restraints to which I could not submit. *This* man is not disagreeable to me; but if I must enter the connubial state, are there not *others,* who may be equally pleasing in their persons, and whose profession may be more conformable to my taste? You, madam, have passed through this scene of trial, with honor and applause. But alas! can your volatile daughter ever acquire your wisdom; ever possess your resolution, dignity and prudence?

I hope soon to converse with you personally upon the subject, and to profit by your precepts and example. I anticipate the hour of my return to your bosom, with impatience. My daily thoughts and nightly dreams restore me to the society of my beloved mamma; and, till I enjoy it in reality, I subscribe myself your dutiful daughter,

ELIZA WHARTON.

LETTER XXI.

TO MISS ELIZA WHARTON.

HARTFORD.

HOW welcome to me, my dear Eliza, are the tidings of your return? My widowed heart has mourned your absence, and languished for the company of its now, dearest connection. When stript of one dependence, the mind naturally collects, and rests itself in another. Your father's death deprived me, for a while, of every enjoyment. But a reviving sense of the duties which I owed to a rising family, roused me from the lethargy of grief. In my cares I found an alleviation of my sorrows. The expanding virtues of my children soothed and exhilerated my drooping spirits; and my attention to their education, and interest, was amply rewarded by their proficiency and duty. In them, every hope, every pleasure now centres. They are the axis on which revolves the temporal felicity of their mother. Judge then, my dear, how anxiously I must watch, how solicitously I must regard every circumstance which relates to their welfare and prosperity! Exquisitely alive to these sensations, your letter awakens my hopes and my fears. As you are young and charming, a thousand dangers lurk unseen around you. I wish you to find a friend and protector, worthy of being rewarded by your love

and your society. Such a one, I think, Mr. Boyer will prove. I am, therefore, sorry, since there can be no other, that his profession should be an objection in your mind. You say, that I have experienced the scenes of trial, connected with that station. I have, indeed; and I will tell you the result of this experience. It is, that I have found it replete with happiness. No class of society has domestic enjoyment more at command, than clergymen. Their circumstances are generally a decent competency. They are removed alike from the perplexing cares of want, and from the distracting parade of wealth. They are respected by all ranks, and partakers of the best company. With regard to its being a dependent situation, what one is not so? Are we not all links in the great chain of society, some more, some less important; but each upheld by others, throughout the confederated whole? In whatever situation we are placed, our greater or less degree of happiness must be derived from ourselves. Happiness is in a great measure the result of our own dispositions and actions. Let us conduct uprightly and justly; with propriety and steadiness; not servilely cringing for favor, nor arrogantly claiming more attention and respect than our due; let us bear with fortitude the providential, and unavoidable evils of life, and we shall spend our days with respectability and contentment, at least.

I will not expatiate on the topic of your letter, till we have a personal interview, for which I am, indeed, impatient. Return, my daughter, as soon as politeness will allow, to your expecting friends; more especially, to the fond embraces of your affectionate mother,

M. WHARTON.

Letter XXII.

TO MISS ELIZA WHARTON.

HAMPSHIRE.

CAN time, can distance, can absence allay, or extinguish the sentiments of refined affection, the ardor of true love? No, my dear Eliza. If I may judge by my own heart, I shall say they cannot. Amidst the parade which has attended me, the interesting scenes in which I have been engaged, and the weighty cares, which have occupied my attention, your idea has been the solace of my retired moments; the soother of every anxious thought. I recal, with pleasure, the conversation which we have shared. I dwell with rapture on the marks of favor which I have received from you. My first wish is the continuance and increase of these favors; my highest ambition, to deserve them. I look forward and anticipate with impatience, the future enjoyment of your society; and hope we shall one day experience the reality of those beautiful lines of Thompson:

> ———"An elegant sufficiency,
> Content, retirement, rural quiet, friendship;
> Books, ease and alternate labor, useful life;
> Progressive virtue, and approving heaven;
> These are the matchless joys of virtuous love."

Mr. Selby, my particular friend, will have the honor of delivering this letter. He will be able to give you any information, relative to our public transactions, which you may wish. May I solicit the favor of a line, through him, in return? It will relieve, in some measure, the tediousness of this separation. I intend to pay my respects to you personally, in about a fortnight; till when, I subscribe myself your sincere and affectionate friend,

J. BOYER.

LETTER XXIII.

TO THE REV. J. BOYER.

NEW-HAVEN.

I HAVE executed your commission, and been amply re-warded for my trouble, by the pleasure I enjoyed in the soci-ety of the agreeable family to which I was introduced; especially of the amiable and accomplished lady, who is the object of your particular regard. I think she fully justifies your partiality to her. She appears to possess both the virtues and the graces. Her form is fine, and her countenance interests us at once in her favor. There is a mixture of dignity and ease, which commands re-spect, and conciliates affection. After these encomiums, will you permit me to say, there is an air of gaiety in her appearance and deportment, which favors a little of coquetry. I am persuaded, however, that she has too much good sense to practice its arts. She received your letter very graciously, asked leave to retire a few moments; and returned with a smile of complacency on her brow, which I construe favorably to you.

There was a Mr. Laurence, with his lady and daughter, and a certain Major Sanford, at the house. The latter, I believe, in the modern sense of the phrase, *is much of a gentleman*, that is, a man of show and fashion.

Miss Wharton asked me, when I should leave town, and when I should return, or have an opportunity of conveyance to Hampshire? I told her I should write by the next post, and if she had any commands, would be happy to execute them. She would send a line to her friend, she said, if I would take the trou-ble to inclose it in my letter. I readily consented; and told her, that I would call and receive her favor to morrow morning. This chit-chat was a little aside, but I could not but observe, that the foresaid Major Sanford had dropped his part in the conversation

of the rest of the company, and was attending to us, though he endeavored to conceal his attention, by looking carelessly over a play, which lay on the window by him. Yet he evidently watched every word and action of Miss Wharton, as if he were really interested in her movements.

It is said she has many admirers, and I conceive it very possible that this may be one of them; though, truly, I do not think that she would esteem such a conquest any great honor. I now joined in the general topic of conversation, which was politics. Mrs. Richman and Miss Wharton judiciously, yet modestly bore a part; while the other ladies amused themselves with Major Sanford, who was making his sage remarks on the play, which he still kept in his hand. General Richman at length observed, that we had formed into parties. Major Sanford, upon this, laid aside his book. Miss Laurence simpered; and looked as if she was well pleased with being in a party with so fine a man; while her mother replied, that she never meddled with politics; she thought they did not belong to ladies. Miss Wharton and I, said Mrs. Richman, must beg leave to differ from you, madam. We think ourselves interested in the welfare and prosperity of our country; and, consequently, claim the right of inquiring into those affairs, which may conduce to, or interfere with the common weal. We shall not be called to the senate or the field to assert its privileges, and defend its rights, but we shall feel for the honor and safety of our friends and connections, who are thus employed. If the community flourish and enjoy health and freedom, shall we not share in the happy effects? if it be oppressed and disturbed, shall we not endure our proportion of the evil? Why then should the love of our country be a masculine passion only? Why should government, which involves the peace and order of the society, of which we are a part, be wholly excluded from our observation? Mrs. Laurence made some slight reply and waved the subject. The gentlemen applauded Mrs. Richman's sentiments as truly Roman; and what was more, they said, truly republican.

I rose to take leave, observing to Miss Wharton, that I should

call to morrow as agreed. Upon this, Gen. Richman politely requested the favor of my company at dinner. I accepted his invitation, and bid them good night. I shall do the same to you for the present; as I intend, to morrow to scribble the cover, which is to inclose your Eliza's letter.

<div align="right">T. Selby.</div>

Letter XXIV.

TO THE REV. J. BOYER.

<div align="right">NEW-HAVEN.</div>

I RESUME my pen, having just returned from Gen. Richman's; not with an expectation, however, of your reading this, till you have perused, and reperused the inclosed. I can bear such neglect, in this case, as I have been alike interested myself.

I went to Gen. Richman's at twelve o'clock. About a mile from thence, upon turning a corner, I observed a gentleman and lady on horseback, some way before me, riding a very moderate pace, and seemingly in close conversation. I kept at the same distance from them, till I saw them stop at the General's gate. I then put on, and coming up with them, just as they alighted, and was surprised to find them no other than Major Sanford and Miss Wharton. They were both a little disconcerted at my salutation; I know not why. Miss Wharton invited him in; but he declined, being engaged to dine. Gen. Richman received us at the door. As I handed Miss Wharton in, he observed jocosely, that she had changed company. Yes sir, she replied, more than once, since I went out, as you doubtless observed. I was not aware, said Mrs. Richman, that Major Sanford was to be of your party to day. It was quite accidental, madam, said Miss Wharton. Miss Lau-

rence and I had agreed last evening, to take a little airing, this forenoon. A young gentleman, a relation of her's, who is making them a visit, was to attend us. We had not rode more than two miles, when we were overtaken by Major Sanford, who very politely asked leave to join our party. Miss Laurence very readily consented; and we had a very sociable ride. The fineness of the day induced me to protract the enjoyment of it abroad; but Miss Laurence declined riding so far as I proposed, as she had engaged company to dine. We therefore parted till evening, when we are to meet again. What, another engagement! said Mrs. Richman. Only to the assembly, madam. May I inquire after your gallant, my dear? But I have no right, perhaps, to be inquisitive, said Mrs. Richman. Miss Wharton made no reply; and the conversation took a general turn. Miss Wharton sustained her part with great propriety. Indeed, she discovers a fund of useful knowledge, and extensive reading, which render her peculiarly entertaining; while the brilliancy of her wit, the fluency of her language, the vivacity and ease of her manners, are inexpressibly engaging. I am going myself to the assembly this evening, though I did not mention it to General Richman; I therefore took my leave soon after dinner.

I have heard so much in praise of Miss Wharton's penmanship, in addition to her other endowments, that I am almost tempted to break the seal of her letter to you; but I forbear. Wishing you much happiness in the perusal of it, and more in the possession of its writer, I subscribe myself, yours, &c.

T. SELBY.

LETTER XXV.

TO THE REV. J. BOYER.

Sir,

YOUR favor of the 4th inst.* came to hand yesterday. I received it with pleasure, and embrace this early opportunity of contributing my part to a correspondence, tending to promote a friendly and social intercourse. An epistolary communication between the sexes has been with some, a subject of satire and censure; but unjustly, in my opinion. With persons of refinement and information, it may be a source of entertainment and utility. The knowledge and masculine virtues of your sex may be softened, and rendered more diffusive by the inquisitiveness, vivacity, and docility of ours; drawn forth and exercised by each other.

In regard to the *particular* subject of your's I shall be silent. Ideas of that kind are better conveyed, on my part, by words, than by the pen.

I congratulate you on your agreeable settlement, and hope it will be productive of real and lasting happiness. I am convinced that felicity is not confined to any particular station, or condition in life; yet methinks some are better calculated to afford it to me, than others.

Your extract from a favorite poet is charmingly descriptive; but is it not difficult to ascertain what we can pronounce "an elegant sufficiency?" Perhaps you will answer as some others have done, We can attain it by circumscribing our wishes within the compass of our abilities. I am not very avaricious; yet I must own that I should like to enjoy it without so much trouble as that would cost me.

*Instant; of the current month—ed.

Excuse my seeming levity. You have flattered my cheerfulness by commending it; and must, therefore, indulge me in the exercise of it. I cannot conveniently be at the pains of restraining its sallies, when I write in confidence.

Is a sprightly disposition, in your view, indicative of a giddy mind, or an innocent heart? Of the latter, I presume; for I know you are not a misanthrope.

We expect the pleasure of Mr. Selby's company to dinner. You are, certainly, under obligations to his friendship for the liberal encomiums he bestowed on you, and your prospects yesterday. Mrs. Richman rallied me after he was gone, on my listening ear. The General and she unite in requesting me to present their respects. Wishing you health and happiness, I subscribe myself your friend,

ELIZA WHARTON.

LETTER XXVI.

TO MISS LUCY FREEMAN.

NEW-HAVEN.

I AM perplexed and embarrassed, my friend, by the assiduous attentions of this Major Sanford. I shall write circumstantially, and frankly to you, that I may have the benefit of your advice. He came here, last Monday, in company with Mr. Laurence, his wife, and daughter, to make us a visit. While they were present, a Mr. Selby, a particular friend of Mr. Boyer, came in, and delivered me a letter from him. I was really happy in the reception of this proof of his affection. His friend gave a very flattering account of his situation and prospects.

The watchful eye of Major Sanford traced every word and action, respecting Mr. Boyer, with an attention, which seemed to

border on anxiety. That, however, did not restrain, but rather accellerate my vivacity and inquisitiveness on the subject; for I wished to know whether it would produce any real effect upon him, or not.

After Mr. Selby's departure, he appeared pensive, and thoughtful, the remainder of the evening; and evidently sought an opportunity of speaking to me aside; which I studiously avoided. Miss Laurence and I formed an engagement to take an airing in the morning on horseback; attended by a relation of hers, who is now with them. They called for me about ten, when we immediately set out upon our preconcerted excursion. We had not proceeded far, before we were met by Major Sanford. He was extremely polite, and finding our destination was not particular, begged leave to join our party. This was granted, and we had an agreeable tour for several miles; the time being passed in easy, and unstudied remarks upon obvious occurrences. Maj. Sanford could not, however, conceal his particular attention to me, which rather nettled Miss Laurence. She grew somewhat serious, and declined riding so far as we had intended; alledging that she expected company to dine.

Major Sanford understanding that she was going to the assembly in the evening with Mr. Gordon, solicited me to accept a ticket and form a party with them. The entertainment was alluring, and I consented. When we had parted with Miss Laurence, Major Sanford insisted on my riding a little farther; saying, he must converse with me on a particular subject; and if I refused him this opportunity, that he must visit me, at my residence, let it offend whom it would. I yielded to his importunity; and we rode on. He then told me that his mind was in a state of suspense and agitation, which was very painful to bear; and which I only could relieve; that my cheerful reception of Mr. Boyer's letter, yesterday, and deportment respecting him, had awakened in his breast all the pangs of jealousy, which the most ardent love could feel; that my treatment of Mr. Boyer's friend convinced him that I was more interested in his affairs than I was willing to own; that he foresaw himself to be condemned to an

eternal separation; and the total loss of my favor and society, as soon as time and circumstances would allow.

His zeal, his pathos, alarmed me. I begged him to be calm. To you, said I, as a friend, I have intrusted my situation in relation to Mr. Boyer. You know that I am under no special obligation to him; and I do not intend to form any immediate connection. Mr. Boyer must have different ideas, madam; and he has reason for them, if I may judge by appearances. When do you expect another visit from him? In about a fortnight. And is my fate to be then decided; and so decided, as I fear it will be, through the influence of your friends, if not by your own inclination? My friends, sir, will not control; they will only advise to what they think most for my interest; and I hope, that my conduct will not be unworthy of their approbation. Pardon me, my dear Eliza, said he, if I am impertinent; it is my regard for you which impels me to the presumption. Do you intend to give your hand to Mr. Boyer? I do not intend to give my hand to any man at present. I have but lately entered society; and wish, for a while, to enjoy my freedom, in the participation of pleasures, suited to my age and sex. These, said he, you are aware, I suppose, when you form a connection with that man, you must renounce; and content yourself with a confinement to the tedious round of domestic duties, the pedantic conversation of scholars, and the invidious criticisms of a whole town. I have been accustomed, said I, and am therefore attached to men of letters; and as to the praise or censure of the populace, I hope always to enjoy that approbation of conscience, which will render me superior to both. But you forget your promise, not to talk in this style; and have deviated far from the character of a friend and brother, with which you consented to rest satisfied. Yes, but I find myself unequal to the task. I am not stoic enough, tamely to make so great a sacrifice. I must plead for an interest in your favor, till you banish me from your presence, and tell me plainly that you hate me. We had by this time reached the gate; and as we dismounted, were unexpectedly accosted by Mr. Selby, who had come agreeably to his promise, to dine with us, and receive my letter to Mr. Boyer.

Major Sanford took his leave as General Richman appeared at the door. The General and his lady rallied me on my change of company; but very prudently concealed their sentiments of Major Sanford, while Mr. Selby was present. Nothing material occurred before, and during dinner; soon after which, Mr. Selby went away. I retired to dress for the assembly; and had nearly completed the labor of the toilet, when Mrs. Richman entered. My friendship for you, my dear Eliza, said she, interests me so much in your affairs, that I cannot repress my curiosity to know who has the honor of your hand, this evening. If it be any honor, said I, it will be confered on Major Sanford. I think it far too great to be thus bestowed, returned she. It is perfectly astonishing to me, that the virtuous part of my sex will countenance, caress, and encourage those men, whose profession it is to blast their reputation, destroy their peace, and triumph in their infamy! Is this, madam, the avowed design of Major Sanford? I know not what he avows; but his practice too plainly bespeaks his principles and views. Does he now practice the arts you mention; or do you refer to past follies? I cannot answer for his present conduct; his past has established his character. You, madam, are an advocate for charity; that, perhaps, if exercised in this instance might lead you to think it possible for him to reform; to become a valuable member of society; and, when connected with a lady of virtue and refinement, to be capable of making a good husband. I cannot conceive that such a lady would be willing to risk her all upon the slender prospect of his reformation. I hope the one with whom I am conversing, has no inclination to so hazardous, an experiment. Why, not much. Not much! If you have any, why do you continue to encourage Mr. Boyer's addresses? I am not sufficiently acquainted with either yet, to determine which to take. At present, I shall not confine myself in any way. In regard to these men, my fancy and my judgment are in scales. Sometimes one preponderates, sometimes the other. Which will finally outweigh, time alone can reveal. O my cousin, beware of the delusions of fancy! Reason must be our guide, if we would expect durable happiness. At this instant a servant opened the

door, and told me that Major Sanford waited in the parlor. Being
ready, I wished Mrs. Richman a good evening, and went down.
Neither General Richman nor his lady appeared. He therefore
handed me immediately into his phaeton, and we were soon in
the assembly room.

I was surprised, on my entrance, to find Mr. Selby there, as he
did not mention, at dinner, his intention of going. He attached
himself to our party; and, in the intervals of dancing, took every
opportunity of conversing with me. These, however, were not
many; for Major Sanford assiduously precluded the possibility
of my being much engaged by any one else. We passed the eve-
ning very agreeably; but the Major's importunity was rather trou-
blesome, as we returned home. He insisted upon my declaring
whether Mr. Boyer really possessed my affections; and whether
I intended to confer myself on him or not. If, said he, you an-
swer me in the affirmative, I must despair; but if you have not ab-
solutely decided against me, I will still hope, that my persever-
ing assiduity, my faithful love, may at last be rewarded. I told
him that I was under no obligation to give him any account of
my disposition towards another; and that he must remember the
terms of our present association, to which he had subscribed. I
therefore begged him to wave the subject now, if not forever. He
asked my pardon, if he had been impertinent; but desired leave
to renew his request, that I would receive his visits, his friendly
visits. I replied, that I could not grant this; and that he must
blame himself, not me, if he was an unwelcome guest at General
Richman's. He lamented the prejudices which my friends had
imbibed against him; but flattered himself that I was more liberal
than to be influenced by them, without any positive proof of de-
merit; as it was impossible that his conduct towards me should
ever deviate from the strictest rules of honor and love.

What shall I say now, my friend? This man, to an agreeable
person has superadded, graceful manners, an amiable temper,
and a fortune sufficient to ensure the enjoyments of all the pleas-
ing varieties of social life. Perhaps a gay disposition, and a lax
education may have betrayed him into some scenes of dissipa-

tion. But is it not an adage generally received, that "*a reformed rake makes the best husband?*" My fancy leads me for happiness to the festive haunts of fashionable life. I am at present, and know not but I ever shall be, too volatile for a confinement to domestic avocations, and sedentary pleasures. I dare not, therefore, place myself in a situation where these must be indispensable. Mr. Boyer's person, and character are agreeable. I really esteem the man. My reason and judgment, as I have observed before, declare for a connection with him, as a state of tranquillity and rational happiness. But the idea of relinquishing those delightful amusements and flattering attentions, which wealth and equipage bestow, is painful. Why were not the virtues of the one, and the graces and affluence of the other combined? I should then have been happy indeed! But, as the case now stands, I am loath to give up either; being doubtful which will conduce most to my felicity.

Pray write me impartially; let me know your real sentiments, for I rely greatly upon your opinion. I am, &c.

ELIZA WHARTON.

LETTER XXVII.

TO THE REV. MR. BOYER.

NEW-HAVEN.

I AM quite a convert to Pope's assertion, that "Every woman is, at heart, a rake." How else can we account for the pleasure which they evidently receive from the society, the flattery, the caresses of men of that character? Even the most virtuous of them seem naturally prone to gaiety, to pleasure, and, I had almost said, to dissipation! How else shall we account for the existence of this disposition, in your favorite fair? It cannot be the result of

her education. Such a one as she has received, is calculated to give her a very different turn of mind. You must forgive me, my friend, for I am a little vexed, and alarmed on your account. I went last evening to the assembly, as I told you in my last that I intended. I was purposely without a partner, that I might have the liberty to exercise my gallantry, as circumstances should invite. Indeed, I must own, that my particular design was, to observe Miss Wharton's movements, being rather inclined to jealousy in your behalf. She was handed into the assembly room by Major Sanford. The brilliance of their appearance, the levity of their manners, and the contrast of their characters I found to be a general subject of speculation. I endeavored to associate with Miss Wharton, but found it impossible to detach her a moment from the coxcomb who attended her. If she has any idea of a connection with you, why does she continue to associate with another, especially with one of so opposite a description? I am seriously afraid, that there is more intimacy between them, than there ought to be, considering the encouragement she has given you.

I hope you will not be offended by my freedom in this matter. It originates in a concern for your honor and future happiness. I am anxious, lest you should be made the dupe of a coquette, and your peace of mind fall a sacrifice to an artful debauchee. Yet I must believe, that Miss Wharton has, in reality, all that virtue and good sense of which she enjoys the reputation; but her present conduct is mysterious.

I have said enough (more than I ought, perhaps) to awaken your attention to circumstances, which *may* lead to important events. If they appear of little, or no consequence to you, you will at least ascribe the mention of them to motives of sincere regard, in your friend and humble servant,

T. SELBY.

LETTER XXVIII.

TO MR. CHARLES DEIGHTON.

NEW-HAVEN.

I GO on finely with my amour. I have every encouragement that I could wish. Indeed my fair one does not verbally declare in my favor; but then, according to the vulgar proverb, *that actions speak louder than words,* I have no reason to complain; since she evidently approves my gallantry, is pleased with my company, and listens to my flattery. Her sagatious friends have undoubtedly given her a detail of my vices. If, therefore, my past conduct has been repugnant to her notions of propriety, why does she not act consistently, and refuse at once to associate with a man whose character she cannot esteem? But no; that, Charles, is no part of the female plan: our entrapping a few of their sex, only discovers the gaiety of our dispositions, the insinuating graces of our manners, and the irresistible charms of our persons and address. These qualifications are very alluring to the sprightly fancy of the fair. They think to enjoy the pleasures which result from this source; while their vanity and ignorance prompt each one to imagine herself superior to delusion; and to anticipate the honor of reclaiming the libertine, and reforming the rake! I dont know, however, but this girl will really have that merit with me; for I am so much attached to her, that I begin to suspect I should sooner become a convert to sobriety than lose her. I cannot find that I have made much impression on her heart as yet. Want of success in this point mortifies me extremely, as it is the first time I ever failed. Besides, I am apprehensive that she is prepossessed in favor of the other swain, the clerical lover, whom I have mentioned to you before. The chord, therefore, upon which I play the most, is the dissimilarity of their dispositions and pleasures. I endeavor to detach her from him, and dis-

affect her towards him; knowing, that if I can separate them entirely, I shall be more likely to succeed in my plan. Not that I have any thoughts of marrying her myself; that will not do at present. But I love her too well to see her connected with another for life. I must own myself a little revengeful too in this affair. I wish to punish her friends, as she calls them, for their malice towards me; for their cold and negligent treatment of me whenever I go to the house. I know that to frustrate their designs of a connection between Mr. Boyer and Eliza would be a grievous disappointment. I have not yet determined to seduce her, though, with all her pretensions to virtue, I do not think it impossible. And if I should, she can blame none but herself, since she knows my character, and has no reason to wonder if I act consistently with it. If she will play with a lion, let her beware of his paw, I say. At present, I wish innocently to enjoy her society; it is a luxury which I never tasted before. She is the very soul of pleasure. The gayest circle is irradiated by her presence, and the highest entertainment receives its greatest charm from her smiles. Besides, I have purchased the seat of Capt. Pribble, about a mile from her mother's; and can I think of suffering her to leave the neighborhood, just as I enter it? I shall exert every nerve to prevent that, and hope to meet with the usual success of

<div style="text-align: right;">PETER SANFORD.</div>

LETTER XXIX.

TO MISS ELIZA WHARTON.

HARTFORD.

YOU desire me to write to you, my friend; but if you had not, I should by no means have refrained. I tremble at the precipice on which you stand; and must echo, and re-echo the seasonable admonition of the excellent Mrs. Richman, "Beware of the delusions of fancy!" You are strangely infatuated by them! Let not the magic arts of that worthless Sanford lead you, like an *ignis fatuus* from the path of rectitude and virtue!

I do not find, in all your conversations with him, that one word about marriage drops from his lips. This is mysterious? No, it is characteristic of the man. Suppose, however, that his views are honorable; yet what can you expect, what can you promise yourself from such a connection? "A reformed rake," you say, "makes the best husband;" a trite, but a very erroneous maxim, as the fatal experience of thousands of our sex can testify. In the first place, I believe that rakes very seldom *do* reform, while their fortunes and constitutions enable them to pursue their licentious pleasures. But even allowing this to happen, can a woman of refinement and delicacy enjoy the society of a man, whose mind has been corrupted, whose taste has been vitiated, and who has contracted a depravity both of sentiment and manners, which no degree of repentance can wholly efface? Besides, of true love they are absolutely incapable. Their passions have been too much hackneyed to admit so pure a flame. You cannot anticipate sincere and lasting respect from them. They have been so long accustomed to the company of those of our sex, who observe no esteem; that the greatest dignity and purity of character can never excite it in their breasts. They are naturally prone to jealousy. Habituated to an intercourse with the baser

part of the sex, they level the whole, and seldom believe any to be incorruptible. They are always hard hearted and cruel. How else could they triumph in the miseries which they frequently occasion? Their specious manners may render them agreeable companions abroad; but at home the evil propensities of their minds will invariably predominate. They are steeled against the tender affections, which render domestic life delightful; strangers to the kind, the endearing sympathies of husband, father, and friend! The thousand nameless attentions which soften the rugged path of life, are neglected; and deemed unworthy of notice by persons who have been innured to scenes of dissipation and debauchery! and is a man of this description to be the partner, the companion, the bosom friend of my Eliza? Forbid it heaven! Let not the noble qualities, so lavishly bestowed upon her, be thus unworthily sacrificed!

You seem to be particularly charmed with the fortune of Major Sanford; with the gaiety of his appearance; with the splendor of his equipage; with the politeness of his manners; with what you call the graces of his person! These, alas! are superficial, ensnaring endowments. As to fortune, prudence, economy, and regularity are necessary to preserve it, when possessed. Of these Major Sanford is certainly destitute; unless common fame (which more frequently tells truth than some are willing to allow) does him great injustice. As to external parade, it will not satisfy the rational mind, when it aspires to those substantial pleasures for which yours is formed. And as to the graces of person and manners, they are but a wretched substitute for those virtues which adorn and dignify human life. Can you, who have always been used to serenity and order in a family, to rational, refined and improving conversation, relinquish them, and launch into the whirlpool of frivolity, where the correct taste and the delicate sensibility which you possess must constantly be wounded by the frothy and illiberal sallies of licentious wit?

This, my dear, is but a faint picture of the situation to which you seem inclined! Reverse the scene, and you will perceive the alternative, which is submitted to your option, in a virtuous con-

nection with Mr. Boyer. Remember that you are acting for life; and that your happiness in this world, perhaps in the next, depends on your present choice!

I called, last evening, to see your mamma. She is fondly anticipating your return, and rejoicing in the prospect of your agreeable and speedy settlement. I could not find it in my heart to distress her by intimating that you had other views. I wish her benevolent bosom never more to feel the pangs of disappointed hope.

I am busily engaged in preparing for my nuptials. The solemn words "as long as ye both shall live," render me thoughtful and serious. I hope for your enlivening presence soon; which will prove a seasonable cordial to the spirits of your

LUCY FREEMAN.

LETTER XXX.

TO MISS LUCY FREEMAN.

NEW-HAVEN.

I BELIEVE your spirits need a cordial indeed, my dear Lucy; after drawing so dreadful a portrait of my swain. But I call him mine no longer. I renounce him entirely. My friends shall be gratified. And if their predictions are verified, I shall be happy in a union with the man of their choice. General Richman and lady have labored abundantly to prove that my ruin was inevitable if I did not immediately break all intercourse with Major Sanford. I promised a compliance with their wishes; and have accomplished the task, though a hard one I found it. Last Thursday he was here, and desired leave to spend an hour with me. I readily consented, assuring my friends it should be the last hour, which I would ever spend in his company.

He told me that he was obliged to leave town for a few days; and, as I should probably see Mr. Boyer, before his return, he could not depart in peace without once more endeavoring to interest me in his favor; to obtain some token of esteem, some glimpse of hope, that I would not utterly reject him, to support him in his absence. I thanked him for the polite attention he had paid me, since our acquaintance; told him that I should ever retain a grateful sense of his partiality to me; that he would ever share my best wishes; but that all connection of the kind, to which he alluded, must from that time, for ever cease.

He exerted all his eloquence to obtain a retraction of that sentence, and ran, with the greatest volubility, through all the protestations, prayers, entreaties, professions and assurances which love could feel or art contrive. I had resolution, however, to resist them, and to command my own emotions on the occasion, better than my natural sensibility gave me reason to expect.

Finding every effort vain, he rose precipitately, and bade me adieu. I urged his tarrying to tea; but he declined, saying, that he must retire to his chamber, being, in his present state of mind, unfit for any society, as he was banished from mine. I offered him my hand, which he pressed with ardor to his lips, and bowing in silence, left the room.

Thus terminated this affair; an affair, which, perhaps, was only the effect of mere gallantry on his part, and of unmeaning pleasantry on mine; and which, I am sorry to say, has given my friends so much anxiety and concern. I am under obligations to them for their kind solicitude, however causeless it may have been.

As an agreeable companion, as a polite and finished gallant, Major Sanford is all that the most lively fancy could wish. And as you have always affirmed that I was a little inclined to coquetry, can you wonder at my exercising it upon so happy a subject? Besides, when I thought more seriously, his liberal fortune was extremely alluring to me, who, you know, have been hith-

erto confined to the rigid rules of prudence and economy, not to say, necessity in my finances.

Miss Laurence called on me yesterday, as she was taking the air, and asked me whether Major Sanford took leave of me when he left town? He was here last week, said I, but I did not know that he was gone away. O yes, she replied, he is gone to take possession of his seat, which he has lately purchased of Captain Pribble. I am told it is superb; and it ought to be, if it have the honor of his residence. Then you have a great opinion of Major Sanford, said I. Certainly; and has not every body else? said she. I am sure he is a very fine gentleman. Mrs. Richman smiled rather contemptuously, and I changed the subject.

I believe that the innocent heart of this simple girl is a little taken in.

I have just received a letter from Mr. Boyer, in the usual style. He expects the superlative happiness of kissing my hand next week. O dear! I believe I must begin to fix my phiz.* Let me run to the glass and try if I can make up one that will look *madamish*. Yes, I succeed very well.

I congratulate you on your new neighbor; but I advise friend George to have the guardian knot tied immediately, lest you should be ensnared by his bewitching 'squire.

I have been trying to seduce General Richman to accompany me to the assembly, this evening, but cannot prevail. Were Mrs. Richman able to go with us, he would be very happy to wait on us together; but to tell the truth, he had rather enjoy her company at home, than any which is to be found abroad. I rallied him on his old fashioned taste; but my heart approved and applauded his attachment. I despise the married man or woman, who harbors an inclination to partake of separate pleasures.

I am told, that a servant man inquires for me below; the messenger of some enamoured swain, I suppose. I will step down and learn what message he brings———

Nothing extraordinary; it is only a card of compliments from a

*Facial expression—ed.

Mr. Emmons, a respectable merchant of this city, requesting the honor to wait on me to the assembly this evening. A welcome request, which I made no hesitation to grant. If I must resign these favorite amusements, let me enjoy as large a share as possible, till the time arrive. Adieu. I must repair to the toilet and adorn for a new conquest, the person of

ELIZA WHARTON.

LETTER XXXI.

TO MISS ELIZA WHARTON.

HARTFORD.

I AM very happy to find you are in so good spirits, Eliza, after parting with your favorite swain. For I perceive that he is really the favorite of your fancy, though your heart cannot esteem him; and, independent of that, no sensations can be durable.

I can tell you some news of this strange man. He has arrived, and taken possession of his seat. Having given general invitations, he has been called upon and welcomed by most of the neighboring gentry. Yesterday he made an elegant entertainment. Friend George (as you call him) and I were of the number, who had cards. Twenty one couple went, I am told. We did not go. I consider my time too valuable to be spent in cultivating acquaintance with a person from whom neither pleasure nor improvement are to be expected. His profuseness may bribe the unthinking multitude to show him respect; but he must know, that though

"Places and honors have been bought for gold,
Esteem and love were never to be sold."

I look upon the vicious habits, and abandoned character of Major Sanford, to have more pernicious effects on society, than the perpetrations of the robber and the assassin. These, when detected, are rigidly punished by the laws of the land. If their lives be spared, they are shunned by society, and treated with every mark of disapprobation and contempt. But to the disgrace of humanity and virtue, the assassin of honor; the wretch, who breaks the peace of families, who robs virgin innocence of its charms, who triumphs over the ill placed confidence of the inexperienced, unsuspecting, and too credulous fair, is received, and caressed, not only by his own sex, to which he is a reproach, but even by ours, who have every conceivable reason to despise and avoid him. Influenced by these principles, I am neither ashamed nor afraid openly to avow my sentiments of this man, and my reasons for treating him with the most pointed neglect.

I write warmly on the subject; for it is a subject in which I think the honor and happiness of my sex concerned. I wish they would more generally espouse their own cause. It would conduce to the public weal, and to their personal respectability. I rejoice, heartily, that you have had resolution to resist his allurements, to detect and repel his artifices. Resolution, in such a case, is absolutely necessary; for,

> "In spite of all the virtue we can boast,
> The woman that deliberates is lost."

As I was riding out, yesterday, I met your mamma. She wondered that I was not one of the party at our new neighbor's. The reason, madam, said I, is that I do not like the character of the man. I know nothing of him, said she; he is quite a stranger to me, only as he called at my house, last week, to pay me his respects, as he said, for the sake of my late husband, whose memory he revered; and because I was the mother of Miss Eliza Wharton, with whom he had the honor of some little acquaintance.

His manners are engaging, and I am sorry to hear that his morals are corrupt.

This, my dear, is a very extraordinary visit. I fear that he has not yet laid aside his arts. Be still on your guard, is the advice of your sincere and faithful friend,

LUCY FREEMAN.

LETTER XXXII.

TO MR. CHARLES DEIGHTON.

HARTFORD.

I AM really banished and rejected; desired never more to think of the girl I love, with a view of indulging that love, or of rendering it acceptable to its object! You will perhaps, dispute the propriety of the term, and tell me it is not love, it is only gallantry, and a desire to exercise it with her, as favorite nymph. I neither know, nor care by what appellation you distinguish it, but it truly gives me pain. I have not felt one sensation of genuine pleasure since I heard my sentence; yet I acquiesced in it, and submissively took my leave; though I doubt not but I shall retaliate the indignity one time or other.

I have taken possession of my new purchase, an elegant and delightful residence. It is rendered more so by being in the vicinity of my charmer's native abode. This circumstance will conduce much to my enjoyment, if I can succeed in my plan of separating her from Mr. Boyer. I know that my situation and mode of life are far more pleasing to her than his, and shall therefore trust to my appearance and address for a reestablishment in her favor. I intend, if possible, to ingratiate myself with her particular friends. For this purpose, I called last week at her mother's, to pay my respects to her (so I told the good woman) as an object

of my particular regard; and as the parent of a young lady, whom I had the honor to know and admire. She received me very civilly, thanked me for my attention, and invited me to call whenever I had opportunity; which was the very thing I wanted. I intend likewise, to court popularity. I don't know but I must accept, by and by, some lucrative office in the civil department. Yet I cannot bear the idea of confinement to business. It appears to me quite inconsistent with the character of a gentleman; I am sure it is, with that of a man of pleasure. But something I must do; for I tell you, in confidence, that I was obliged to mortgage this place, because I had not wherewithal to pay for it. But I shall manage matters very well, I have no doubt, and keep up the appearance of affluence, till I find some lady in a strait for a husband, whose fortune will enable me to extricate myself from these embarrassments. Do come and see me, Charles; for, notwithstanding all my gaiety and parade, I have some turns of the hypo, some qualms of conscience, you will call them; but I meddle not with such obsolete words. And so good bye to you, says

PETER SANFORD.

LETTER XXXIII.

TO MISS LUCY FREEMAN.

NEW-HAVEN.

My Dear Friend,

I BELIEVE I must begin to assume airs of gravity; and they will not be quite so foreign to my feelings now, as at some other times. You shall know the reason. I have been associated for three days, with sentiment and sobriety, in the person of Mr.

Boyer. I don't know but this man will seduce me into matrimony. He is very eloquent upon the subject; and his manners are so solemn, that I am strongly tempted, yet I dare not to laugh. Really, Lucy, there is something extremely engaging and soothing too, in virtuous and refined conversation. It is a source of enjoyment which cannot be realised by the dissolute and unreflecting. But then, this particular theme of his, is not a favorite one to me; I mean, as connected with its consequences, care and confinement. However, I have compounded the matter with him, and conditioned that he shall expatiate on the subject, and call it by what name he pleases, *platonic* or *conjugal*, provided he will let me take my own time for the consummation. I have consented that he shall escort me, next week, to see my mamma and my Lucy. O, how the idea of returning to that revered mansion, to those beloved friends, exhilerates my spirits!

General Richman's politeness to me has induced him to invite a large party of those gentlemen and ladies who have been particularly attentive to me, during my residence here, to dine and take tea, to morrow. After that, I expect to be engaged in making farewell visits, till I leave the place. I shall, therefore, forego the pleasure of telling you any occurrences, subsequent to this date, until you see and converse with your sincere friend,

ELIZA WHARTON.

LETTER XXXIV.

TO MRS. RICHMAN.

HARTFORD.

Dear Madam,

THE day after I left your hospitable dwelling, brought me safe to that of my honored mamma; to the seat of maternal and filial affection; of social ease and domestic peace; of every species of happiness which can result from religion and virtue; from refinement in morals, and manners.

I found my brother and his wife, with Lucy Freeman and Mr. Sumner, waiting to receive and bid me welcome. I flew with extacy to the bosom of my mamma, who received me with her accustomed affection, testified by the expressive tears of tenderness which stole silently down her widowed cheek. She was unable to speak. I was equally so. We therefore indulged, a moment, the pleasing emotions of sympathising sensibility. When disengaged from her fond embrace, I was saluted by the others in turn; and having recovered myself, I presented Mr. Boyer to each of the company, and each of the company to him. He was cordially received by all, but more especially by my mamma.

The next day I was called upon and welcomed by several of my neighboring acquaintance; among whom I was not a little surprised to see Major Sanford. He came in company with Mr. Stoddard and Lady, whom he overtook, as he told me, near by; and, as they informed him that the design of their visit was to welcome me home, he readily accepted their invitation to partake of the pleasure which every one must receive on my return. I bowed slightly at his compliment, taking no visible notice of any peculiarity of expression either in his words or looks.

His politeness to Mr. Boyer, appeared to be the result of habit. Mr. Boyer's to him, to be forced by respect to the company to

which he had gained admission. I dare say, that each felt a conscious superiority; the one on the score of merit; the other on that of fortune. Which ought to outweigh, the judicious mind will easily decide. The scale, as I once observed to you, will turn as fancy or reason preponderates. I believe the esteem which I now have for Mr. Boyer, will keep me steady; except, perhaps, some little excentricities, now and then, just by way of variety. I am going to morrow morning to spend a few days with Lucy Freeman; to assist in the preparation for, and the solemnization of her nuptials. Mr. Boyer, in the mean time, will tarry among his friends in town. My mamma is excessively partial to him; though I am not yet jealous that she means to rival me. I am not certain, however, but it might be happy for him if she should. For I suspect, notwithstanding the disparity of her age, that she is better calculated to make him a good wife than I am or ever shall be.

But to be sober. Please, madam, to make my compliments acceptable to those of your neighbors, whose politeness and attention to me, while at your house, have laid me under particular obligations of gratitude and respect. My best regards attend General Richman. Pray tell him, that though I never expect to be so good a wife as he is blessed with; yet I intend, after a while (when I have sowed all my wild oats) to make a tolerable one.

I am anxious to hear of a wished for event and of your safety. All who know you, feel interested in your health and happiness; but none more warmly than your obliged and affectionate

ELIZA WHARTON.

LETTER XXXV.

TO MISS ELIZA WHARTON.

NEW-HAVEN.

I WRITE a line, at Mrs. Richman's request, just to inform you, Eliza, that yesterday, that lovely and beloved woman presented me with a daughter. This event awakens new sensations in my mind; and calls into exercise a kind of affection which had before lain dormant. I feel already the tenderness of a parent; while imagination fondly traces the mother's likeness in the infant form. Mrs. Richman expects to receive your congratulations, in a letter by the next post. She bids me tell you, moreover, that she hopes soon to receive an invitation, and be able to attend to the consummation you talk of. Give Mrs. Richman's and my particular regards to your excellent mother; and to the worthy Mr. Boyer. With sentiments of esteem and friendship, I am, &c.

S. RICHMAN.

LETTER XXXVI.

TO MRS. RICHMAN.

HARTFORD.

FROM the scenes of festive mirth, from the conviviality of rejoicing friends, and from the dissipating amusements of the gay world, I retire with alacrity, to hail my beloved friend on the important charge which she has received; on the accession to her

family, and, may I not say, on the addition to her care; since that care will be more than counterbalanced by the pleasure it confers. Hail happy babe! Ushered into the world by the best of mothers; entitled by birth-right to virtue and honor; defended by parental love, from the weakness of infancy and childhood, by guardian wisdom from the perils of youth, and by affluent independence from the griping hand of poverty, in more advanced life! May these animating prospects be realised by your little daughter; and may you long enjoy the rich reward of seeing her all that you wish!

Yesterday, my dear friend, Lucy Freeman gave her hand to the amiable and accomplished Mr. George Sumner. A large circle of congratulating friends were present. Her dress was such as wealth and elegance required. Her deportment was every thing that modesty and propriety could suggest. They are, indeed, a charming couple. The consonance of their dispositions, the similarity of their tastes, and the equality of their ages are a sure pledge of happiness. Every eye beamed with pleasure on the occasion, and every tongue echoed the wishes of benevolence. Mine only was silent. Though not less interested in the felicity of my friend than the rest, yet the idea of a separation; perhaps, of an alienation of affection, by means of her entire devotion to another, cast an involuntary gloom over my mind. Mr. Boyer took my hand, after the ceremony was past. Permit me, Miss Wharton, said he, to lead you to your lovely friend; her happiness must be heightened by your participation of it. Oh no; said I, I am too selfish for that. She has conferred upon another that affection which I wished to engross. My love was too fervent to admit a rival. Retaliate then, said he, this fancied wrong, by doing likewise. I observed that this was not a proper time to discuss that subject; and, resuming my seat, endeavored to put on the appearance of my accustomed vivacity. I need not relate the remaining particulars of the evening's entertainment. Mr. Boyer returned with my mamma, and I remained at Mrs. Freeman's.

We are to have a ball here, this evening. Mr. Boyer has been

with us, and tried to monopolize my company; but in vain. I am too much engaged by the exhilerating scenes around, for attending to a subject which affords no variety. I shall not close this till to morrow.

————I am rather fatigued with the amusements of last night, which were protracted to a late hour. Mr. Boyer was present; and I was pleased to see him not averse to the entertainment, though his profession prevented his taking an active part. As all the neighboring gentry were invited, Mr. Freeman would, by no means, omit Major Sanford, which his daughter earnestly solicited. It happened (unfortunately, shall I say?) that I drew him for a partner. Yet I must own, that I felt very little reluctance to my lot. He is an excellent dancer, and well calculated for a companion in the hours of mirth and gaiety. I regretted Mr. Boyer's being present, however; because my enjoyment seemed to give him pain. I hope he is not inclined to the passion of jealousy. If he is, I fear it will be somewhat exercised.

Lucy Freeman, now Mrs. Sumner, removes, next week, to Boston. I have agreed to accompany her, and spend a month or two in her family. This will give variety to the journey of life. Be so kind as to direct your next letter to me there.

Kiss the dear little babe for me. Give love, compliments, &c. as respectively due; and believe me, with every sentiment of respect, your affectionate

ELIZA WHARTON.

LETTER XXXVII.

TO MR. CHARLES DEIGHTON.

HARTFORD.

Dear Charles,

MY hopes begin to revive. I am again permitted to associate with my Eliza; invited to the same entertainment! She does not refuse to join with me in the mazy dance, and partake the scenes of festive mirth. Nay, more; she allows me to press her hand to my lips; and listens to the sighing accents of love. Love her, I certainly do. Would to heaven I could marry her! Would to heaven I had preserved my fortune; or she had one to supply its place! I am distracted at the idea of losing her forever. I am sometimes tempted to solicit her hand in serious earnest; but if I should, poverty and want must be the consequence. Her disappointment in the expectation of affluence and splendor, which I believe her ruling passion, would afford a perpetual source of discontent and mutual wretchedness.

She is going to Boston with her friend, Mrs. Sumner. I must follow her. I must break the connection, which is rapidly forming, between her and Mr. Boyer; and enjoy her society a while longer, if no more.

I have had a little intimation from New-Haven, that Miss Laurence is partial to me, and might easily be obtained, with a handsome property into the bargain. I am neither pleased with, nor averse to the girl. But she has money, and that may supply the place of love, by enabling me to pursue independent pleasures. This she must expect, if she marries a man of my cast. She doubtless knows my character; and if she is so vain of her charms or influence, as to think of reforming or confining me, she must bear the consequences.

However, I can keep my head up, at present, without re-

course to the noose of matrimony; and shall, therefore, defer any particular attention to her, till necessity requires it.

I am, &c.

PETER SANFORD.

LETTER XXXVIII.

TO MRS. M. WHARTON.

BOSTON.

YOU commanded me, my dear mamma, to write you. That command, I cheerfully obey, in testimony of my ready submission and respect. No other avocation could arrest my time, which is now completely occupied in scenes of amusement.

Mrs. Sumner is agreeably settled and situated. She appears to be possessed of every blessing which can render life desirable. Almost every day, since our arrival, has been engrossed by visitants. Our evenings, we have devoted to company abroad; and that more generally than we should otherwise have done, as my stay is limited to so short a period. The museum, the theatres, the circus and the assemblies have been frequented.

Mrs. Sumner has made me several presents, notwithstanding which, the articles requisite to a fashionable appearance, have involved me in considerable expense. I fear that you will think me extravagant when you are told how much.

Mr. Boyer tarried in town about a week, having business. He appeared a little concerned at my taste for dissipation, as he once termed it. He even took the liberty to converse seriously on the subject.

I was displeased with his freedom; and reminded him that I had the disposal of my own time, as yet; and that while I es-

caped the censure of my own heart, I hoped that no one else would presume to arraign it. He apologised, and gave up his argument.

I was much surprised, the first time I went to the play, to see Major Sanford in the very next box. He immediately joined our party; and wherever I have been since, I have been almost sure to meet him.

Mr. Boyer has taken his departure; and I do not expect to see him again, till I return home.

O mamma! I am embarrassed about this man. His worth I acknowledge; nay, I esteem him very highly. But can there be happiness with such a disparity of dispositions?

I shall soon return to the bosom of domestic tranquillity, to the arms of maternal tenderness, where I can deliberate and advise at leisure, about this important matter. Till when,

 I am, &c.

 ELIZA WHARTON.

LETTER XXXIX.

TO MR. T. SELBY.

<div align="right">HAMPSHIRE.</div>

Dear Sir,

I BELIEVE that I owe you an apology for my long silence. But my time has been much engrossed of late; and my mind much more so. When it will be otherwise, I cannot foresee. I fear, my friend, that there is some foundation for your suspicions respecting my beloved Eliza. What pity it is, that so fair a form, so accomplished a mind, should be tarnished, in the smallest degree, by the follies of coquetry! If this be the fact, which I

am loth to believe, all my regard for her shall never make me the dupe of it.

When I arrived at her residence, at New-Haven, where, I told you in my last, I was soon to go, she gave me a most cordial reception. Her whole behavior to me was correspondent with those sentiments of esteem and affection which she modestly avowed. She permitted me to accompany her to Hartford, to restore her to her mother, and to declare my wish to receive her again from her hand. Thus far, all was harmony and happiness. As all my wishes were consistent with virtue and honor, she readily indulged them. She took apparent pleasure in my company, encouraged my hopes of a future union, and listened to the tender accents of love.

But the scenes of gaiety, which invited her attention, reversed her conduct. The delightful hours of mutual confidence, of sentimental converse, and of the interchange of refined affection, were no more! Instead of these, parties were formed, unpleasing to my taste; and every opportunity was embraced to join in diversions, in which she knew I could not consistently take a share. I, however, acquiesced in her pleasure, though I sometimes thought myself neglected, and even hinted it to her mother. The old lady apologised for her daughter, by alledging that she had been absent for a long time; that her acquaintances were rejoiced at her return, and welcomed her by striving to promote her amusement.

One of her most intimate friends was married during my stay; and she appeared deeply interested in the event. She spent several days in assisting her, previous to the celebration. I resided, in the mean time, at her mamma's, visiting her at her friend's, where Major Sanford, among others, was received as a guest. Mrs. Sumner acquainted me that she had prevailed on Miss Wharton to go and spend a few weeks with her at Boston, whither she was removing; and urged my accompanying them. I endeavored to excuse myself, as I had been absent from my people a considerable time, and my return was now expected. But

their importunity was so great, and Eliza's declaration that it would be very agreeable to her, so tempting, that I consented. Here I took lodgings and spent about a week, taking every opportunity to converse with Eliza, striving to discover her real disposition towards me. I mentioned the inconvenience of visiting her so often as I wished, and suggested my desire to enter, as soon as might be, into a family relation. I painted in the most alluring colours the pleasures resulting from domestic tranquillity, mutual confidence, and conjugal affection; and insisted on her declaring frankly whether she designed to share this happiness with me, and when it should commence. She owned that she intended to give me her hand; but when she should be ready, she could not yet determine. She pretended a promise from me to wait her time; to consent that she should share the pleasures of the fashionable world, as long as she chose, &c.

I then attempted to convince her of her mistaken ideas of pleasure; that the scenes of dissipation, of which she was so passionately fond, afforded no true enjoyment; that the adulation of the coxcomb could not give durability to her charms, or secure the approbation of the wise and good; nor could the fashionable amusements of brilliant assemblies, and crouded* theatres furnish the mind with

> "That which nothing earthly gives, or can destroy,
> The soul's calm sunshine, and the heart felt joy."

These friendly suggestions, I found were considered as the theme of a priest; and my desire to detach her from such empty pursuits, as the selfishness of a lover. She was even offended at my freedom; and warmly affirmed, that no one had a right to arraign her conduct. I mentioned Major Sanford who was then in town, and who (though she went to places of public resort with Mr. and Mrs. Sumner) always met and gallanted her home. She rallied me upon my jealousy, as she termed it; wished that I would attend her myself, and then she should need no other gallant. I answered that I had rather resign that honor to another;

*Crowded—ed.

but wished, for her sake, that he might be a gentleman whose character would not disgrace the company with which he associated. She appeared mortified and chagrined in the extreme. However, she studiously suppressed her emotions; and even soothed me with the blandishments of female softness. We parted amicably. She promised to return soon, and prepare for a compliance with my wishes. I cannot refuse to believe her! I cannot cease to love her! My heart is in her possession. She has a perfect command of my passions. Persuasion dwells on her tongue. With all the boasted fortitude and resoultion of our sex, we are but mere machines. Let love once pervade our breasts; and its object may mould us into any form that pleases her fancy, or even caprice.

I have just received a letter from Eliza, informing me of her return to Hartford. To morrow I shall set out on a visit to the dear girl; for, my friend, notwithstanding all her foibles, she is very dear to me. Before you hear from me again, I expect that the happy day will be fixed; the day which shall unite, in the most sacred bands, this lovely maid, and your faithful friend,

J. BOYER.

LETTER XL.

TO MR. T. SELBY.

HAMPSHIRE.

I HAVE returned; and the day, indeed, is fixed; but Oh! how different from my fond expectations! It is not the day of union, but the day of final separation; the day which divides me from my charmer; the day which breaks asunder the bands of love; the day on which my reason assumes its empire, and triumphs over the arts of a finished coquette! Congratulate me, my

friend, that I have thus overcome my feelings, and repelled the infatuating wiles of a deceitful girl. I would not be understood to impeach Miss Wharton's virtue; I mean her chastity. Virtue in the common acceptation of the term, as applied to the sex, is confined to that particular, you know. But in my view, this is of little importance, where all other virtues are wanting!

When I arrived at Mrs. Wharton's, and inquired for Eliza, I was told that she had rode out; but was soon expected home. An hour after, a phaeton stopped at the door, from which my fair one alighted, and was handed into the house by Major Sanford, who immediately took leave. I met her and offered my hand, which she received with apparent tenderness.

When the family had retired after supper, and left us to talk on our particular affairs, I found the same indecision, the same loathness to bring our courtship to a period, as formerly. Her previous excuses were renewed, and her wishes to have a union still longer delayed, were zealously urged. She could not bear the idea of confinement to the cares of a married life at present; and begged me to defer all solicitation on that subject to some future day. I found my temper rise, and told her plainly, that I was not thus to be trifled with; that if her regard for me was sincere; if she really intended to form a connection with me, she could not thus protract the time, try my patience, and prefer every other pleasure to the rational interchange of affection, to the calm delights of domestic life. But in vain did I argue against her false notions of happiness; in vain did I represent the dangerous system of conduct, which she now pursued, and urge her to accept, before it was too late, the hand and heart which were devoted to her service. That, she said, she purposed, ere long to do; and hoped amply to reward my faithful love; but she could not fix the time this evening. She must consider a little further; and likewise consult her mother. Is it not Major Sanford whom you wish to consult, madam? said I. She blushed, and gave me no answer. Tell me, Eliza, I continued, tell me frankly, if he has not supplanted me in your affections; if he be not the cause of my being thus evasively, thus cruelly treated? Major Sanford,

sir, replied she, has done you no harm. He is a particular friend of mine; a polite gentleman, and an agreeable neighbor; and therefore I treat him with civility; but he is not so much interested in my concerns, as to alter my disposition towards any other person. Why, said I, do you talk of friendship with a man of his character? Between his society and mine, there is a great contrast. Such opposite pursuits and inclinations cannot be equally pleasing to the same taste. It is therefore necessary, that you renounce the one, to enjoy the other. I will give you time to decide which. I am going to a friend's house to spend the night; and will call on you to morrow, if agreeable, and converse with you further upon the matter. She bowed assent, and I retired.

The next afternoon I went as agreed; and found her mamma and her alone in the parlor. She was very pensive and appeared to have been in tears. The sight affected me. The idea of having treated her harshly, the evening before, disarmed me of my resolution to insist on her decision that day. I invited her to ride with me and visit a friend, to which she readily consented. We spent our time agreeably. I forebore to press her on the subject of our future union; but strove rather to soothe her mind, and inspire her with sentiments of tenderness towards me. I conducted her home, and returned early in the evening to my friend's, who met me at the door; and jocosely told me, that he expected I should now rob them of their agreeable neighbor. But, added he, we have been apprehensive that you would be rivalled, if you delayed your visit much longer. I did not suspect a rival, said I. Who can the happy man be? I can say nothing from personal observation, said he; but fame, of late, has talked loudly of Major Sanford and Miss Wharton. Be not alarmed, continued he, seeing me look grave. I presume no harm is intended. The Major is a man of gallantry, and Miss Wharton is a gay lady; but I dare say that your connection will be happy, *if it be formed.* I noticed a particular emphasis on the word *if;* and as we were alone, I followed him with questions, till the whole affair was developed. I informed him of my embarrassment; and he gave me to understand that Eliza's conduct had, for some time past, been a

subject of speculation in the town; that formerly, her character was highly esteemed; but that her intimacy with a man of Sanford's known libertinism; more especially as she was supposed to be engaged to another, had rendered her very censurable; that they were often together; that wherever she went, he was sure to follow, as if by appointment; that they walked, talked, sung and danced together in all companies; that some supposed he would marry her; others, that he only meditated adding her name to the black catalogue of deluded wretches, whom he had already ruined!

I rose, and walked the room in great agitation. He apologized for his freedom; was sorry if he had wounded my feelings; but friendship alone had induced him frankly to declare the truth, that I might guard against duplicity and deceit.

I thanked him for his kind intensions; and assured him that I should not quit the town till I had terminated this affair, in one way or another.

I retired to bed, but sleep was a stranger to my eyes. With the dawn I rose; and after breakfast walked to Mrs. Wharton's, who informed me, that Eliza was in her chamber, writing to a friend, but would be down in a few minutes. I entered into conversation with the old lady on the subject of her daughter's conduct; hinted my suspicions of the cause, and declared my resolution of knowing my destiny immediately. She endeavored to extenuate, and excuse her as much as possible; but frankly owned that her behavior was mysterious; that no pains had been wanting, on her part, to alter and rectify it; that she had remonstrated, expostulated, advised and entreated, as often as occasion required. She hoped that my resolution would have a good effect, as she knew that her daughter esteemed me very highly.

In this manner we conversed till the clock struck twelve; and Eliza, not appearing, I desired her mamma to send up word that I waited to see her. The maid returned with an answer that she was indisposed, and had lain down. Mrs. Wharton observed, that she had not slept for several nights, and complained of the head ache in the morning. The girl added, that she would wait

on Mr. Boyer in the evening. Upon this information I rose and abruptly took my leave. I went to dine with a friend, to whom I had engaged myself the day before; but my mind was too much agitated to enjoy either the company or the dinner. I excused myself from tarrying to tea, and returned to Mrs. Wharton's. On inquiry, I was told that Eliza had gone to walk in the garden; but desired that no person might intrude on her retirement. The singularity of the request awakened my curiosity, and determined me to follow her. I sought her in vain, in different parts of the garden, till, going towards an arbor, almost concealed from sight, by surrounding shrubbery, I discovered her, sitting in close conversation with Major Sanford! My blood chilled in my veins, and I stood petrified with astonishment, at the disclosure of such baseness and deceit. They both rose in visible confusion. I dared not trust myself to accost them. My passions were raised, and I feared that I might say or do something unbecoming my character. I therefore gave them a look of indignation and contempt, and retreated to the house. I traversed the parlor hastily, overwhelmed with chagrin and resentment! Mrs. Wharton inquired the cause. I attempted to tell her, but my tongue refused utterance! While in this situation, Eliza entered the room. She was not less discomposed than myself. She sat down at the window and wept. Her mamma wept likewise. At length she recovered herself, in a degree, and desired me to sit down. I answered no; and continued walking. Will you, said she, permit me to vindicate my conduct and explain my motives? Your conduct, said I, cannot be vindicated; your motives need no explanation; they are too apparent! How, Miss Wharton, have I merited this treatment from you? But I can bear it no longer. Your indifference to me proceeds from an attachment to another; and forgive me, if I add, to one, who is the disgrace of his own sex, and the destroyer of yours. I have been too long the dupe of your dissimulation and coquetry. Too long has my peace of mind been sacrificed to the arts of a woman, whose conduct has proved her unworthy of my regard; insensible to love, gratitude and honor!

To you, madam, said I, turning to her mother, I acknowledge

my obligations for your friendship, politeness and attention. I once hoped for the privilege of rocking for you the cradle of declining age. I am deprived of that privilege; but I pray that you may never want a child, whose love and duty shall prove a source of consolation and comfort!

Farewell! If we never meet again in this life, I hope and trust we shall in a better; where the parent's eye shall cease to weep for the disobedience of a child; and the lover's heart to bleed for the infidelity of his mistress!

I turned to Eliza, and attempted to speak; but her extreme emotion softened me, and I could not command my voice. I took her hand, and bowing, in token of an adieu, went precipitately out of the house. The residence of my friend, with whom I lodged, was at no great distance, and thither I repaired. As I met him in the entry, I rushed by him, and betook myself to my chamber.

The fever of resentment, and the tumult of passion began now to give place to the softer emotions of the soul. I found myself perfectly unmanned. I gave free scope to the sensibility of my heart; and the effeminate relief of tears materially lightened the load which oppressed me.

After this arduous struggle I went to bed; and slept more calmly than for several nights before. The next morning I wrote a farewell letter to Eliza (a copy of which I shall inclose to you) and ordering my horse to be brought, left town immediately.

My resentment of her behavior has much assisted me in erasing her image from my breast. In this exertion I have succeeded beyond my most sanguine expectations. The more I reflect on her temper and disposition, the more my gratitude is enlivened towards the wise Disposer of all events for enabling me to break asunder the snares of the deluder. I am convinced, that the gaiety and extravagance of her taste, the frivolous levity of her manners disqualify her for the station in which I wished to have placed her. These considerations, together with that resignation to an overruling Providence which the religion I profess, and teach, requires me to cultivate, induce me cheerfully to adopt the following lines of an ingenious poet:

"Since all the downward tracts of time,
 God's watchful eye surveys,
Oh, who so wise to choose our lot,
 Or regulate our ways?

Since none can doubt his equal love,
 Unmeasurably kind,
To his unerring gracious will,
 Be every wish resign'd.

Good, when he gives, supremely good,
 Not less when he denies;
E'en crosses from his sovereign hand,
 Are blessings in disguise."

I am, &c.

 J. BOYER.

TO MISS ELIZA WHARTON.

Enclosed in the foregoing.

 HARTFORD.

Madam,

FEARING, that my resolution may not be proof against the eloquence of those charms, which have so long commanded me, I take this method of bidding you a final adieu. I write not as a lover. That connection between us is for ever dissolved; but I address you as a friend; a friend to your happiness, to your reputation, to your temporal and eternal welfare. I will not rehearse the innumerable instances of your imprudence and misconduct, which have fallen under my observation. Your own heart must be your monitor! Suffice it for me to warn you against the dangerous tendency of so dissipated a life; and to tell you that I have traced (I believe aright) the cause of your dissimulation and indifference to me. They are an aversion to the sober, rational, frugal mode of living, to which my profession leads; a fondness for the parade, the gaiety, not to say, the licentiousness of a station calculated to gratify such a disposition; and a prepossession for Ma-

jor Sanford, infused into your giddy mind by the frippery, flattery and artifice of that worthless and abandoned man. Hence you preferred a connection with him, if it could be accomplished; but a doubt, whether it could, together with the advice of your friends, who have kindly espoused my cause, have restrained you from the avowal of your real sentiments, and led you to continue your civilities to me. What the result of your coquetry would have been, had I waited for it, I cannot say, nor have I now any desire or interest to know. I tear from my breast the idea which I have long cherished of future union and happiness with you in the conjugal state. I bid a last farewell to these fond hopes, and leave you for ever!

For your own sake, however, let me conjure you to review your conduct, and before you have advanced beyond the possibility of returning to rectitude and honor, to restrain your steps from the dangerous path in which you now tread!

Fly Major Sanford. That man is a deceiver. Trust not his professions. They are certainly insincere; or he would not affect concealment; he would not induce you to a clandestine intercourse! Many have been the victims of his treachery! O Eliza! add not to the number! Banish him from your society, if you wish to preserve your virtue unsullied, your character unsuspicious! It already begins to depreciate. Snatch it from the envenomed tongue of slander, before it receive an incurable wound!

Many faults have been visible to me; over which my affection once drew a veil. That veil is now removed. And, acting the part of a disinterested friend, I shall mention some few of them with freedom. There is a levity in your manners, which is inconsistent with the solidity and decorum becoming a lady who has arrived to years of discretion. There is also an unwarrantable extravagance betrayed in your dress. Prudence and economy are such necessary, at least, such decent virtues, that they claim the attention of every female, whatever be her station or her property. To these virtues you are apparently inattentive. Too large a portion of your time is devoted to the adorning of your person.

Think not that I write thus plainly from resentment. No; it is

from benevolence. I mention your foibles, not to reproach you with them, but that you may consider their nature and effects, and renounce them.

I wish you to regard this letter as the legacy of a friend; and to improve it accordingly. I shall leave town before you receive it. O, how different are my sensations at going, from what they were when I came! but I forbear description.

Think not, Eliza, that I leave you with indifference! The conflict is great; the trial is more than I can calmly support! Yet the consciousness of duty, affords consolation. A duty I conceive it to be, which I owe to myself; and to the people of my charge, who are interested in my future connection.

I wish not for an answer; my resolution is unalterably fixed. But should you hereafter be convinced of the justice of my conduct; and become a convert to my advice, I shall be happy to hear it.

That you may have wisdom to keep you from falling, and conduct you safely through this state of trial to the regions of immortal bliss, is the fervent prayer of your sincere friend, and humble servant,

<div style="text-align:right">J. BOYER.</div>

LETTER XLI.

TO MRS. LUCY SUMNER.

<div style="text-align:right">HARTFORD.</div>

THE retirement of my native home is not so gloomy, since my return from Boston, as I expected, from the contrast between them.

Indeed, the customs and amusements of this place are materially altered, since the residence of Major Sanford among us. The

dull, old fashioned sobriety which formerly prevailed, is nearly banished; and cheerfulness, vivacity, and enjoyment are substituted in its stead. Pleasure is now diffused through all ranks of the people, especially the rich; and surely it ought to be cultivated, since the wisest of men informs us, that "a merry heart doth good like a medicine." As human life has many diseases, which require medicines, are we not right in selecting the most agreeable and palatable? Major Sanford's example has had great influence upon our society in general; and though some of our old dons think him rather licentious; yet, for ought I can see, he is as strict an observer of decorum, as the best of them. True, he seldom goes to church; but what of that? The Deity is not confined to temples made with hands. He may worship him as devoutly elsewhere, if he chuses; and who has a right to say he does not?

His return from Boston was but a day or two after mine. He paid me an early visit; and, indeed, has been very attentive ever since. My mamma is somewhat precise in her notions of propriety; and of course, blames me for associating so freely with him. She says, that my engagements to Mr. Boyer ought to render me more sedate; and more indifferent to the gallantry of mere *pleasure-hunters*, to use her phrase. But I think otherwise. If I am to become a recluse, let me, at least, enjoy those amusements, which are suited to my taste, a short time first. Why should I refuse the polite attentions of this gentleman? They smoothe the rugged path of life, and wonderfully accelerate the lagging wheels of time.

Indeed, Lucy, he has an admirable talent for contributing to vary, and increase amusement. We have few hours unimproved. Some new plan of pleasure, and sociability is constantly courting our adoption. He lives in all the magnificence of a prince; and why should I, who can doubtless share that magnificence if I please, forego the advantages and indulgences it offers, merely to gratify those friends who pretend to be better judges of my happiness than I am myself.

I have not yet told my mamma that he entertains me with the

lover's theme; or, at least, that I listen to it. Yet I must own to you, from whom I have never concealed an action or idea, that his situation in life charms my imagination; that the apparent fervor and sincerity of his passion affect my heart. Yet there is something extremely problematical in his conduct. He is very urgent with me to dissolve my connection with Mr. Boyer, and engage not to marry him without his consent; or knowledge, to say no more. He warmly applauds my wish, still longer to enjoy the freedom and independence of a single state; and professedly adopts it for his own. While he would disconnect me from another, he mysteriously conceals his own intentions and views. In conversation with him yesterday, I plainly told him that his conduct was unaccountable; that if his professions and designs were honorable he could not neglect to mention them to my mamma; that I should no longer consent to carry on a clandestine intercourse with him; that I hourly expected Mr. Boyer, whom I esteemed, and who was the favorite of my friends; and that unless he acted openly in this affair before his arrival, I should give my hand to him.

He appeared thunderstruck at this declaration. All his words and actions were indicative of the most violent emotions of mind. He entreated me to recall the sentence; for I knew not, he said, his motives for secrecy; yet he solemnly swore that they were honorable. I replied in the words of the poet,

> "Trust not a man, they are by nature cruel,
> False, deceitful, treacherous, and inconstant.
> When a man talks of love, with caution hear him;
> But if he swear, he'll certainly deceive you."

He begged that he might know by what means he had provoked my suspicions; by what means he had forfeited my confidence? His importunity vanquished my fortitude; and before we parted, I again promised to make him acquainted, from time to time, with the progress of my connection with Mr. Boyer.

Now, my dear friend, I want your advice more than ever. I am inadvertently embarrassed by this man; and how to extricate my-

self, I know not. I am sensible that the power is in my hands; but the disposition (shall I confess it) is wanting!

> "I know the right, and I approve it too;
> I know the wrong, and yet the wrong pursue!"

I have just received a card from Major Sanford, inviting me to ride this afternoon. At first I thought of returning a negative answer; but recollecting that Mr. Boyer must soon be here, I concluded it best to embrace this opportunity, of talking further with him. I must now prepare to go; but shall not close this letter, for I intend writing in continuation, as events occur, till this important business is decided.

Tuesday evening. The little tour which I mentioned to you this afternoon, was not productive of a final determination. The same plea was repeated over, and over again, without closing the cause. On my return I found Mr. Boyer waiting to receive me. My heart beat an involuntary welcome. I received him very cordially, though with a kind of pleasure mixed with apprehension. I must own that his conversation and manners are much better calculated to bear the scrutinising eye of a refined understanding and taste, than Major Sanford's. But whether the fancy ought not to be consulted about our settlement for life, is with me a question.

When we parted last, I had promised Mr. Boyer, to inform him positively, at this visit, when my hand should be given. He therefore came, as he told me in the course of our conversation, with the resolution of claiming the fulfilment of this promise.

I begged absolution; told him, that I could not possibly satisfy his claim; and sought still to evade, and put off the important decision. He grew warm; and affirmed that I treated him ungenerously, and made needless delays. He even accused me of indifference towards him; and of partiality to another. Major Sanford he believed, was the man who robbed him of the affection which he had supposed his due. He warned me against any intercourse with him, and insisted that I must renounce the society of the one or the other immediately. He would leave me, he said,

this evening and call to morrow to know the result of my determination. It was late before he bade me good night; since which I have written these particulars. It is now time to lay aside my pen, and deliberate what course to take.

Wednesday Evening. Last night I closed not my eyes. I rose this morning with the sun, and went into the garden till breakfast. My mamma doubtless saw the disorder of my mind, but kindly avoided any inquiry about it. She was affectionately attentive to me, but said nothing of my particular concerns. I mentioned not my embarrassment to her. She had declared herself in favor of Mr. Boyer; therefore I had no expectation, that she would advise impartially. I retired to my chamber, and remained in a kind of reverie, for more than an hour; when I was roused by the rattling of a carriage at the door. I hastened to the window, and saw Major Sanford just driving away. The idea of his having been to converse with my mamma, gave me new sensations. A thousand perplexities occurred to my mind relative to the part most proper for me to act in this critical situation. All these might have been avoided, had I gone down and inquired into the matter; but this I delayed till dinner. My mamma then informed me, that Major Sanford had been with her, and inquired for me; but that she thought it unnecessary to call me, as she presumed I had no particular business with him. I knew the motives by which she was actuated, and was vexed at her evasions. I told her plainly, that she would never carry her point in this way; that I thought myself capable of conducting my own affairs; and wished her not to interfere, except by her advice, which I should always listen to, and comply with when I could possibly make it consistent with my inclination and interest. She wept at my undutiful anger (of which I have severely repented since) and affectionately replied, that my happiness was the object of her wishes and prayers; conformably to which she felt constrained, freely to speak her mind, though it incurred my displeasure. She then went through again with all the comparative circumstances and merits of the two candidates for my favor, which have perpetually rung in my ears for months. I shed tears

at the idea of my embarrassment; and in this condition Mr. Boyer found us. He appeared to be affected by my visible disorder; and without inquiring the cause, endeavored to dissipate it. This was kindly done. He conversed upon indifferent subjects; and invited me to ride, and take tea with your mamma, to which I readily consented. We found her at home; and passed the time agreeably, excepting the alloy of your absence. Mr. Boyer touched lightly on the subject of our last evening's debate; but expatiated largely on the pleasing power of love; and hoped that we should one day both realize and exemplify it in perfection. When we returned, he observed that it was late, and took his leave; telling me that he should call to morrow; and begged that I would then relieve his suspense. As I was retiring to bed, the maid gave me a hint that Major Sanford's servant had been here and left a letter. I turned instantly back to my mamma, and telling her my information, demanded the letter. She hesitated, but I insisted on having it; and seeing me resolute, she reluctantly gave it into my hand. It contained the following words:

"Am I forsaken? Am I abandoned? Oh my adorable Eliza, have you sacrificed me to my rival? Have you condemned me to perpetual banishment, without a hearing?

I came this day, to plead my cause at your feet; but was cruelly denied the privilege of·seeing you! My mind is all anarchy and confusion! My soul is harrowed up with jealousy! I will be revenged on those who separate us, if that distracting event take place! But it is from your lips only that I can hear my sentence! You must witness its effects! To what lengths my despair may carry me, I know not! You are the arbitress of my fate!

Let me conjure you to meet me in your garden to morrow at any hour you shall appoint. My servant will call for an answer in the morning. Deny me not an interview; but have pity on your faithful *Sanford."*

I wrote for answer, that I would meet him to morrow, at five o'clock in the afternoon.

I have now before me another night for consideration; and shall pass it in that employment. I purpose not to see Mr. Boyer, till I have conversed with Major Sanford.

Thursday Morning. The morning dawns, and ushers in the day; a day, perhaps big with the fate of your friend! What that fate may be is wrapped in the womb of futurity; that futurity which a kind Providence has wisely concealed from the penetration of mortals!

After mature consideration; after revolving and re-revolving every circumstance on both sides of the question, I have nearly determined, in compliance with the advice of my friends, and the dictates of my own judgment, to give Mr. Boyer the preference, and with him to tread the future round of life.

As to the despair of Major Sanford, it does not much alarm me. Such violent passions are seldom so deeply rooted, as to produce lasting effects. I must, however, keep my word, and meet him according to promise.

Mr. Boyer is below. My mamma has just sent me word that he wished to see me. My reply was that I had lain down, which was a fact.

One o'Clock. My mamma, alarmed by my indisposition, has visited my apartment. I soon convinced her that it was but trifling, owing principally to the want of sleep; and that an airing in the garden, which I intended towards night, would restore me.

Ten o'clock, at night. The day is past! and such a day it has been, as I hope never more to see!

At the hour appointed, I went tolerably composed and resolute into the garden. I had taken several turns, and retired into the little arbor, where you and I have spent so many happy hours, before Major Sanford entered. When he appeared, a consciousness of the impropriety of this clandestine intercourse suffused my cheek, and gave a coldness to my manners. He immediately penetrated the cause, and observed that my very countenance told him he was no longer a welcome guest to me. I asked him if he ought so to be; since his motives for seeking admission,

were unworthy of being communicated to my friends? That he said was not the case, but that prudence in the present instance required a temporary concealment.

He then undertook to exculpate himself from blame, assuring me that as soon as I should discountenance the expectations of Mr. Boyer, and discontinue the reception of his address, his intentions should be made known. He was enlarging upon this topic, when we heard a footstep approaching us; and looking up saw Mr. Boyer within a few paces of the arbor.—Confusion seized us both! We rose involuntarily from our seats, but were mute as statues! He spoke not a word, but casting a look of indignant accusation at me, a glance which penetrated my very soul, turned on his heel, and walked hastily back to the house.

I stood a few moments, considering what course to take, though shame and regret had almost taken from me the power of thought.

Major Sanford took my hand. I withdrew it from him. I *must* leave you, said I. Where will you go? said he. I will go and try to retrieve my character. It has suffered greatly by this fatal interview.

He threw himself at my feet and exclaimed, leave me not, Eliza, I conjure you not to leave me. Let me go now, I rejoined, or I bid you farewell for ever. I flew precipitately by him, and went into the parlor, where I found Mr. Boyer and my mamma, the one traversing the room in the greatest agitation; the other in a flood of tears! Their appearance affected me; and I wept like an infant! when I had a little recovered myself, I begged him to sit down; He answered no. I then told him, that however unjustifiable my conduct might appear, perhaps I might explain it to his satisfaction, if he would hear me; that my motives were innocent, though they doubtless wore the aspect of criminality, in his view. He sternly replied, that no palliation could avail; that my motives were sufficiently notorious! He accused me of treating him ill, of rendering him the dupe of coquetting artifice, of having an intrigue with Major Sanford, and declared his determination to leave me for ever, as unworthy of his regard, and incapa-

ble of love, gratitude, or honor!—There was too much reason in support of his accusations for me to gainsay them, had his impetuosity suffered me to attempt it.

But in truth I had no inclination to self defence. My natural vivacity had forsaken me; and I listened without interrupting him to the fluency of reproachful language, which his resentment inspired. He took a very solemn and affectionate leave of my mamma; thanking her for her politeness, and wishing her much future felicity. He attempted to address me, I suppose somewhat in the same way, but his sensibility overcame him; and he only took my hand, and bowing in silence, departed.

The want of rest for two long nights together, the exercise of mind, and conflict of passions, which now tortured my breast, were too much for me to support!

When I saw that he was gone; that he had actually forsaken me, I fainted. My mamma, with the assistance of the maid, soon restored me.

When I opened my eyes, and beheld this amiable and tender parent, watching and attending me with the most anxious concern; without one reproachful word, without one accusing look, my reflections upon the part I had acted, in defeating her benevolent wishes, were exquisitely afflictive! But we mutually forbore to mention the occasion of my illness; and I complied with her advice to take some refreshment, and retire to my chamber. I am so much fatigued by the exertions of the day, that rest is absolutely necessary; and I lay aside my pen to seek it.

Friday Morning. When I shall again receive the balmy influence of sleep, I know not. It has absolutely forsaken me at present. I have had a most restless night. Every awakening idea presented itself to my imagination; whether I had sustained a real loss in Mr. Boyer's departure; reflections on my own misconduct, with the censure of my friends, and the ill-natured remarks of my enemies, excited the most painful anxiety in my mind!

I am going down, but how shall I see my mamma? To her will I confess my faults, in her maternal breast repose my cares, and

by her friendly advice regulate my conduct. Had I done this be-
fore, I might have escaped this trouble, and saved both her and
myself many distressing emotions!

Friday Evening. I have had a long conversation with my
mamma, which has greatly relieved my mind. She has soothed
me with the most endearing tenderness.

Mr. Atkins, with whom Mr. Boyer lodged, while in town,
called here this afternoon. I did not see him, but he told my
mamma that Mr. Boyer had returned home, and left a letter for
me, which he had promised to convey with his own hand. By this
letter I am convinced that the dye is absolutely cast, with respect
to him, and that no attempts on my part to bring about a reconcilia-
tion would be either prudent or successful. He has penetrated the
cause of my proceedings; and such is his resentment, that I am in-
clined not much to regret his avoiding another interview.

My excuses would be deemed utterly insufficient, and truth
would not befriend and justify me.

As I know you are impatient to hear from me, I will now dis-
patch this long letter without any other addition, than that I am
your sincere friend,

ELIZA WHARTON.

LETTER XLII.

TO MR. CHARLES DEIGHTON.

HARTFORD.

WELL, Charles, the show is over, as we yankees say; and
the girl is my own. That is, if I will have her. I shall take
my own time for that, however. I have carried my point, and am
amply revenged on the whole posse of those dear friends of
hers. She was entangled by a promise (not to marry this priest

without my knowledge,) which her conscience would not let her break. Thank God, I have no conscience. If I had, I believe it would make wretched work with me! I suppose she intended to have one, or the other of us; but preferred me. I have escaped the noose, this time, and I'll be fairly hanged, if I ever get so near it again. For indeed Charles, I was seriously alarmed. I watched all their motions; and the appearances of harmony between them awakened all my activity and zeal. So great was my infatuation, that I verily believe I should have asked her in marriage, and risked the consequences, rather than to have lost her!

I went to the house, while Mr. Boyer was in town, but her mamma refused to call her, or to acquaint her that I was there. I then wrote a despairing letter, and obtained a conference with her in the garden. This was a fortunate event for me. True, Eliza was very haughty, and resolutely insisted on immediate declaration or rejection. And I cannot say what would have been the result, if Mr. Boyer had not surprized us together. He gave us a pretty harsh look and retired without speaking a word.

I endeavored to detain Eliza, but in vain. She left me on my knees, which are always ready to bend on such occasions.

This finished the matter, it seems. I rose, and went into a near neighbor's to observe what happened; and in about half an hour saw Mr. Boyer come out, and go to his lodgings.

This, said I to myself, is a good omen. I went home, and was informed next day, that he had mounted his horse and departed.

I heard nothing more of her till yesterday, when I determined to know how she stood affected towards me. I therefore paid her a visit, her mamma being luckily abroad.

She received me very placidly, and told me, on inquiry, that Mr. Boyer's resentment at her meeting me in the garden was so great, that he had bid her a final adieu. I congratulated myself on having no rival; hoped that her favor would now be unbiassed, and that in due time I should reap the reward of my fidelity. She begged me not to mention the subject; said she had been perplexed by our competition, and wished not to hear any thing fur-

ther about it at present. I bowed in obedience to her commands and changed the discourse.

I informed her, that I was about taking a tour to the southward; that I should be absent several months, and trusted that on my return her embarrassments would be over.

I left her with regret. After all, Charles, she is the *summum bonum* of my life. I must have her in some way or other. No body else shall, I am resolved.

I am making preparations for my journey; which between you and me, is occasioned by the prospect of making a speculation, by which I hope to mend my affairs. The voyage will at least lessen my expenses, and screen me from the importunity of creditors till I can look about me.

<div align="right">PETER SANFORD.</div>

LETTER XLIII.

TO MISS ELIZA WHARTON.

<div align="right">NEW-HAVEN.</div>

My Dear Eliza,

THROUGH the medium of my friends at Hartford I have been informed of the progress of your affairs, as they have transpired. The detail which my sister gave me of your separation from Mr. Boyer was painful; as I had long contemplated a happy union between you. But still more disagreeable sensations possessed my breast, when told that you had suffered your lively spirits to be depressed, and resigned yourself to solitude and dejection!

Why, my dear friend, should you allow this event thus to affect you? Heaven, I doubt not, has happiness still in store for you—perhaps greater than you could have enjoyed in that con-

nection. If the conviction of any misconduct on your part, give you pain, dissipate it by the reflection, that unerring rectitude is not the lot of mortals, that few are to be found who have not deviated in a greater or less degree from the maxims of prudence. Our greatest mistakes may teach lessons which will be useful through life.

But I will not moralize. Come and see us; and we will talk over the matter once, and then dismiss it for ever. Do prevail on your mamma to part with you a month or two at least. I wish you to witness how well I manage my nursery business. You will be charmed with little Harriot. I am already enough of the mother to think her a miniature of beauty and perfection.

How natural, and how easy the transition from one stage of life to another! Not long since I was a gay, volatile girl; seeking satisfaction in fashionable circles and amusements; but now I am thoroughly domesticated. All my happiness is centered within the limits of my own walls; and I grudge every moment that calls me from the pleasing scenes of domestic life. Not that I am so selfish as to exclude my friends from my affection or society. I feel interested in their concerns, and enjoy their company. I must own, however, that conjugal and parental love are the main springs of my life. The conduct of some mothers in depriving their helpless offspring of the care and kindness which none but a mother can feel, is to me unaccountable. There are many nameless attentions which nothing short of maternal tenderness, and solicitude can pay; and for which the endearing smiles, and progressive improvements of the lovely babe are an ample reward.

How delightful to trace from day to day the expansion of reason and the dawnings of intelligence! Oh, how I anticipate the time, when these faculties shall be displayed by the organs of speech; when the lisping accent shall heighten our present pleasure, and the young idea be capable of direction "how to shoot"! General Richman is not less interested by these enjoyments than myself. All the father beams in his eye! All the husband reigns in his heart, and pervades his every action!

Miss Lawrence is soon to be married to Mr. Laiton. I believe he is a mere fortune-hunter. Indeed she has little to recommend her to any other. Nature has not been very bountiful, either to her body, or mind. Her parents have been shamefully deficient in her education; but have secured to her what they think the chief good; not considering that happiness is by no means the invariable attendant of wealth.

I hope this incoherent scroll will amuse, while it induces you speedily to favor us with another visit.

My best wishes attend your honored mamma, while I subscribe myself, &c.

A. RICHMAN.

LETTER XLIV.

TO MRS. LUCY SUMNER.

HARTFORD.

I AM extremely depressed, my dear Lucy! The agitating scenes, through which I have lately passed, have broken my spirits, and rendered me unfit for society.

Major Sanford has visited me, and taken his leave. He is gone to the southward on a tour of two or three months. I declined any further conversation with him, on the subject of love. At present, I wish not to hear it mentioned by any one.

I have received a very friendly and consolatory letter from Mrs. Richman. She invites me to spend a few months with her; which with my mamma's consent I shall do. I hope the change of situation and company will dissipate the gloom which hangs over my mind.

It is a common observation, that we know not the value of a blessing but by deprivation.

This is strictly verified in my case. I was insensible of my regard for Mr. Boyer, till this fatal separation took place. His merit and worth now appear in the brightest colors. I am convinced of that excellence which I once slighted; and the shade of departed happiness haunts me perpetually! I am sometimes tempted to write him, and confess my faults; to tell him the situation of my mind, and to offer him my hand. But he has precluded all hopes of success, by the severity of his letter to me. At any rate, I shall do nothing of the kind, till my return from New Haven.

I am the more willing to leave home, as my affairs are made a town talk. My mamma persuades me to disregard it. But how can I rise superior to "The world's dread laugh, which scarce the firm philosopher can scorn?"

Pray remember me to Mr. Sumner. You are happy, my friend, in the love and esteem of a worthy man; but more happy still, in deserving them. Adieu.

ELIZA WHARTON.

LETTER XLV.

TO THE SAME.

HARTFORD.

I HAVE returned to the once smiling seat of maternal affection; but I find not repose and happiness, even there!

In the society of my amiable friends at New-Haven, I enjoyed every thing that friendship could bestow; but rest to a disturbed mind was not in their power.

I was on various parties of pleasure, and passed through different scenes of amusement; but with me they have lost their charms. I relished them not as formerly.

Mrs. Richman advises me to write to Mr. Boyer, and I have

concluded to act accordingly. If it answer no other purpose, it will be a relief to my mind. If he ever felt for me the tenderness and regard which he professed, methinks they cannot be entirely obliterated. If they still remain, perhaps I may rekindle the gentle flame, and we may both be happy. I may at least recal his esteem, and that will be a satisfaction to my conscious mind.

I wonder what has become of Major Sanford! Has he too forsaken me? Is it possible for him wilfully to neglect me? I will not entertain so injurious a suspicion.

Yet, if it were the case, it would not affect me like Mr. Boyer's disaffection; for I frankly own, that my fancy, and a taste for gaity of life, induced me to cherish the idea of a connection with Major Sanford; while Mr. Boyer's real merit has imprinted those sentiments of esteem and love in my heart, which time can never efface.

Instead of two, or three, more than twelve months have elapsed, and I have not received a line from Major Sanford in all that time, which I fully expected, though he made no mention of writing; nor have I heard a syllable about him, except a report circulated by his servants, that he is on the point of marrying, which I do not believe. No, it is impossible! I am persuaded that his passion for me, was sincere, however deceitful he may have been with others. But I will not bestow an anxious thought upon him. My design relative to Mr. Boyer, demands my whole attention.

My hopes and fears alternately prevail, and my resolution is extremely fluctuating. How it finally terminates you shall hear in my next. Pray write to me soon. I stand in need of the consoling power of friendship. Nothing can beguile my pensive hours, and exhilerate my drooping spirits, like your letters.

Let me know how you are to be entertained this winter at the theatre. That, you know, is a favorite amusement of mine. You see I can step out of myself a little. Afford an assisting hand, and perhaps I may again be fit for society.

<div align="right">ELIZA WHARTON.</div>

Letter XLVI.

TO THE REV. J. BOYER.

HARTFORD.

Sir,

IT is partly in compliance with your desire, in your last letter to me, in which you tell me, "that when I am convinced of the justice of your conduct, and become a convert to your advice, you shall be happy to hear it;" and partly from a wish to inform you, that such is in truth my present state of mind, that I now write to you.

I cannot but hope that this letter coming from the hand which you once sought, will not be unacceptable.

Pope very justly observes, "that every year is a critic on the last." The truth of this observation is fully exemplified in my years! How severely this condemns the follies of the preceding, my own heart alone can testify!

I shall not offer any palliation, or apology for my misconduct. You told me it admitted none. I frankly confess it; and if the most humble acknowledgement of my offences, with an assurance that they have cost me the deepest repentance, can in any degree atone for them, I now make that atonement. Casting off the veil of dissimulation, I shall write with frankness; believing you possessed of more honor than to make any ungenerous use of the confidence reposed in you.

To say that I ever esteemed you, may, perhaps, appear paradoxical, when compared with certain circumstances which occurred during our acquaintance; but to assert that I loved you, may be deemed still more so. Yet these are real facts, facts of which I was then sensible, and by which I am now more than ever affected.

I think you formerly remarked, that absence served but to heighten real love. This I find by experience. Need I blush to declare these sentiments, when occasion like this, calls for the avowal? I will go even further, and offer you that heart which once you prized; that hand which you once solicited. The sentiments of affection, which you then cultivated, though suppressed, I flatter myself are not wholly obliterated. Suffer me then to rekindle the latent flame; to revive that friendship and tenderness, which I have so foolishly neglected. The endeavor of my future life shall be to reward your benevolence, and perhaps we may yet be happy together.

But let not this offer of myself constrain you. Let not pity influence your conduct. I would have you return, if that pleasing event take place, a voluntary act. Receive or consent not to confer happiness.

I thought it a duty which I owed to you, and to myself, to make this expiation; this sacrifice of female reserve, for the wrongs I have done you. As such I wish you to accept it; and if your affections are intirely alienated, or otherwise engaged; if you cannot again command the respect and love which I would recal, do not despise me for the concessions I have made. Think as favorably of my past faults, and of my present disposition, as charity will allow. Continue, if possible, to be my friend, though you cease to be my lover.

Should this letter find you in the full possession of happiness, let not the idea of your once loved Eliza, thus intruding itself again upon your thoughts, interrupt your enjoyments. May some distinguished female, as deserving, as fair, partake with you of that bliss which I have forfeited.

Whatever may be my destiny, my best wishes shall ever attend you, and a pleasing remembrance of your honorable attentions preside, till death, in the breast of,

ELIZA WHARTON.

LETTER XLVII.

TO MISS ELIZA WHARTON.

HAMPSHIRE.

Madam,

A S I was sitting last evening in my study, a letter was handed me by a servant; upon which I no sooner cast my eye, than I recognized, with surprise, the hand and seal of my once loved, but to me long lost Eliza! I opened it hastily, and with still greater surprise, read the contents!

You write with frankness. I shall answer in the same manner.

On reviewing our former intercourse, be assured, that I have not an accusing thought in my heart. The regard which I felt for you was tender and animated, but it was not of that passionate kind which ends in death or despair. It was governed by reason, and had a nobler object in view, than mere sensual gratification. It was excited by the appearance of excellent qualities. Your conduct, at length, convinced me it was misplaced; that you possessed not, in reality, those charms which I had fondly ascribed to you. They were inconsistent, I conceived, with that artifice and dissimulation, of which you strove to render me the dupe. But thank heaven, the snare was broken. My eyes were opened to discover your folly; and my heart, engaged, as it was, exerted resolution and strength to burst asunder the chain by which you held me enslaved, and to assert the rights of an injured man.

The parting scene, you remember. I reluctantly bade you adieu. I tore myself from you, determined to eradicate your idea from my breast! Long and severe was the struggle. I at last vanquished, as I thought, every tender passion of my soul, (for they all centered in you) and resigned myself to my God, and my duty; devoting those affections to friendship, which had been disappointed in love. But they are again called into exercise. The

virtuous, the amiable, the accomplished Maria Selby possesses my entire confidence and esteem; and I trust I am not deceived, when I think her highly deserving of both. With her I expect soon to be united in the most sacred and endearing of human relations; with her to pass my future days in serenity and peace.

Your letter, therefore, came too late; were there no other obstacle to the renewal of our connection. I hope at the close of life, when we take a retrospect of the past, that neither of us shall have reason to regret our separation.

Permit me to add, that for your own sake, and for the sake of your ever valued friends, I sincerely rejoice that your mind has regained its native strength and beauty; that you have emerged from the shade of fanciful vanity. For although to adopt your own phrase, I cease to style myself your lover, among the number of your friends, I am happy to be reckoned. As such, let me conjure you, by all that is dear and desirable, both in this life, and another, to adhere, with undeviating exactness, to the path of rectitude and innocence; and to improve the noble talents, which heaven has liberally bestowed upon you, in rendering yourself amiable, and useful to your friends. Thus will you secure your own, while you promote the happiness of all around you.

I shall ever cherish sentiments of kindness towards you, and with gratitude remember your condescension, in the testimony of regard, which you have given me in your last letter.

I hope soon to hear that your heart and hand are bestowed on some worthy man, who deserves the happiness you are formed to communicate. Whatever we may have called errors, will, on my part, be for ever buried in oblivion; and for your own peace of mind, I entreat you to forget that any idea of a connection between us ever existed.

I shall always rejoice at the news of your welfare, and my ardent prayers will daily arise for your temporal and eternal felicity.

I am, &c.

J. Boyer.

Letter XLVIII.

TO MRS. LUCY SUMNER.

HARTFORD.

HEALTH, placid serenity, and every domestic pleasure, are the lot of my friend; while I, who once possessed the means of each, and the capacity of tasting them, have been tossed upon the waves of folly, till I am shipwrecked on the shoals of despair!

Oh my friend, I am undone! I am slighted, rejected by the man who once sought my hand, by the man who still retains my heart! and what adds an insupportable poignancy to the reflection, is self-condemnation! From this inward torture, where shall I flee? Where shall I seek that happiness which I have madly trifled away?

The inclosed letters,* will show you whence this tumult of soul arises. But I blame not Mr. Boyer. He has acted nobly. I approve his conduct, though it operates my ruin!

He is worthy of his intended bride, and she is what I am not, worthy of him. Peace and joy be their portion, both here and hereafter! But what are now my prospects? what are to be the future enjoyments of my life?

Oh that I had not written to Mr. Boyer! by confessing my faults, and by avowing my partiality to him, I have given him the power of triumphing in my distress; of returning to my tortured heart all the pangs of slighted love! and what have I now to console me? my bloom is decreasing; my health is sensibly impaired. Those talents, with the possession of which I have been

*See the two preceding Letters.

flattered, will be of little avail when unsupported by respectability of character!

My mamma, who knows too well the distraction of my mind, endeavors to sooth and compose me, on Christian principles; but they have not their desired effect. I dare not converse freely with her on the subject of my present uneasiness, lest I should distress her. I am therefore, obliged to conceal my disquietude, and appear as cheerful as possible in her company, though my heart is ready to burst with grief!

Oh that you were near me, as formerly, to share and alleviate my cares! to have some friend in whom I could repose confidence, and with whom I could freely converse, and advise, on this occasion, would be an unspeakable comfort!

Such a one, next to yourself, I think Julia Granby to be. With your leave and consent I should esteem it a special favor if she would come and spend a few months with me. My mamma joins in this request. I would write to her on the subject, but cannot compose myself at present. Will you prefer my petition for me?

If I have not forfeited your friendship, my dear Mrs. Sumner, write to me, and pour its healing balm into the wounded mind of your

<div style="text-align: right">ELIZA WHARTON.</div>

LETTER XLIX.

TO MISS ELIZA WHARTON.

BOSTON.

YOUR truly romantic letter came safe to hand. Indeed, my dear, it would make a very pretty figure in a novel. A bleeding heart, slighted love, and all the *et ceteras* of romance, enter into the composition!

Excuse this raillery; and I will now write more seriously. You refer yourself to my friendship for consolation. It shall be exerted for the purpose. But I must act the part of a skilful surgeon, and probe the wound, which I undertake to heal.

Where, O Eliza Wharton! Where is that fund of sense, and sentiment which once animated your engaging form? Where that strength of mind, that independence of soul, that alacrity and sprightliness of deportment, which formerly raised you superior to every adverse occurrence? Why have you resigned these valuable endowments, and suffered yourself to become the sport of contending passions?

You have now emerged from that mist of fanciful folly, which, in a measure obscured the brilliance of your youthful days.

True, you figured among the first rate coquettes; while your friends, who knew your accomplishments, lamented the misapplication of them; but now they rejoice at the returning empire of reason.

True, you have erred; mislead by the gaiety of your disposition, and that volatility, and inconsideration, which were incident to your years; but you have seen, and nobly confessed your errors. Why do you talk of slighted love? True, Mr. Boyer, supposing you disregarded him, transferred his affections to another object; but have you not your admirers still among men of real merit? Are you not esteemed, and caressed by numbers,

who know you capable of shining in a distinguished sphere of life? Turn then, my friend, from the gloomy prospect, which your disturbed imagination has brought into view. Let reason and religion erect their throne in your breast; obey their dictates and be happy. Past experience will point out the quicksands which you are to avoid in your future course.

Date then, from this, a new era of life; and may every moment be attended with felicity. Follow Mr. Boyer's advice, and forget all former connections.

Julia accepts your invitation. Nothing short of your request could induce me to part with her. She is a good girl; and her society will amuse and instruct you.

<div align="right">I am, &c.
LUCY SUMNER.</div>

LETTER L.

TO MRS. LUCY SUMNER.

<div align="right">HARTFORD.</div>

MY Julia Granby has arrived. She is all that I once was; easy, sprightly, debonair. Already has she done much towards relieving my mind. She endeavors to divert, and lead my thoughts into a different channel from that to which they are now prone. Yesterday, we had each an invitation to a ball. She labored hard to prevail on me to go; but I obstinately refused. I cannot yet mix with gay and cheerful circles. I therefore alledged that I was indisposed, and persuaded her to go without me.

The events of my life have always been unaccountably wayward. In many instances I have been ready to suppose that some evil genius presided over my actions, which has directed them contrary to the sober dictates of my own judgment.

I am sometimes tempted to adopt the sentiment expressed in the following lines of the poet,

"To you, great gods, I make my last appeal;
O, clear my conscience, or my crimes reveal!
If wand'ring through the paths of life I've run;
And backward trod the steps, I sought to shun,
Impute my errors to your own decree;
My feet were guilty, but my heart was free."

I suppose you will tell me, that the fate I accuse, through the poet, is only the result of my own imprudence. Well, be it what it may; either the impulse of my own passions, or some higher efficiency; sure I am, that I pay dear for its operation.

I have heard it remarked, that experience is the preceptor of fools; but that the wise need not its instruction. I believe I must be content to rank accordingly, and endeavor to reap advantage from its tuition.

Julia urges me to revisit the scenes of amusements and pleasure; in which she tells me, she is actuated by selfish motives. She wishes it for her own sake. She likes neither to be secluded from them, nor to go alone. I am sometimes half inclined to seck, in festive mirth, a refuge from thought and reflection. I would escape, if possible, from the idea of Mr. Boyer. This I have never been able to accomplish, since he dropped a tear upon my hand, and left me. I marked the spot with my eye; and twenty times in a day, do I view it, and fondly imagine it still there! How could I give him pain! I hope his happy Maria never will! I hope she will reward that merit, which I have slighted! but I forbear. This theme carries away my pen, if I but touch upon it. And no wonder; for it is the sole exercise of my thoughts! Yet I will endeavor to divert them. Send me some new books; not such, however, as will require much attention. Let them be plays or novels, or any thing else, that will amuse and extort a smile.

Julia and I have been rambling in the garden. She insisted upon my going with her into the arbor, where I was surprised

with Major Sanford. What a croud of painful ideas rushed upon my imagination! I believe she repented her rashness. But no more of this. I must lay aside my pen; for I can write nothing else!

<div align="right">ELIZA WHARTON.</div>

LETTER LI.

TO MRS. LUCY SUMNER.

<div align="right">HARTFORD.</div>

Dear Madam,

YOU commanded me to write you respecting Miss Wharton; and I obey. But I cannot describe to you the surprising change, which she has undergone. Her vivacity has entirely forsaken her; and she has actually become, what she once dreaded above all things, a recluse! She flies from company, as eagerly as she formerly sought it! Her mamma is exceedingly distressed by the settled melancholy which appears in her darling child; but neither of us think it best to mention the subject to her. We endeavor to find means to amuse her; and we flatter ourselves that the prospect of success rather increases. It would add greatly to my happiness, to contribute, in any degree, to restore her to herself, to her friends, and to society.

We are all invited to dine abroad to morrow; and to oblige me, she has consented to go.

Pray madam, write to her often. Your letters may do much for her. She is still feelingly alive to the power of friendship; and none can exercise it upon her to greater acceptance, or with more advantage than yourself.

Major Sanford's house is undergoing a complete repair. The re-

port is, that he is soon to be married. Miss Wharton has heard, but does not believe it. I hope, for her sake, it will prove true. For, at any rate, he is about returning; and from her mamma's account of his past conduct towards Eliza, were he to return unconnected, he would probably renew his attentions; and though they might end in marriage, her happiness would not be secured. She has too nice a sense of love and honor, to compound with his licentious principles. A man, who has been dissolute before marriage, will very seldom be faithful afterwards.

I went into Eliza's chamber the other day, and found her with a miniature picture in her hand. You pretend to be a physiognomist, Julia, said she. What can you trace in that countenance? I guessed whose it was; and looking wistfully at it, replied, I believe the original is an artful, designing man. He looks to me like a Chesterfieldian. Pray who is he? Major Sanford, said she; and I am afraid you have hit his character exactly. Sure I am, that the appearance of those traits in it has made my heart ache! She wept, as she spoke it.

Poor girl! I wish he may never give you greater cause to weep! She is strongly blind to the vices and imperfections of this man. Though naturally penetrating, he has some how or other, cast a deceptious mist over her imagination, with respect to himself. She professes neither to love, nor esteem him; and owns that his ungenerous artifice mislead her in her treatment of Mr. Boyer. Yet she has forgiven him, and thinks him a pleasing companion!

How prone to error is the human mind! How much lighter than the breath of zephyrs the operations of fancy! Strange then, it should ever preponderate over the weightier powers of the understanding!

But I will not moralize. My business here is to dissipate, not to collect ideas; and I must regulate myself accordingly.

I am endeavoring to prepare Eliza, by degrees, to accompany me to Boston, the ensuing winter; but think it doubtful whether I shall succeed. I shall, however, return myself; till when, I am, &c.

JULIA GRANBY.

LETTER LII.

TO MISS ELIZA WHARTON.

My Dear Eliza,

I RECEIVED yours of the 24th ult.* and thank you for it; though it did not afford me those lively sensations of pleasure, which I usually feel at the perusal of your letters. It inspired me both with concern, and chagrin. With concern, lest your dejection of mind should affect your health; and with chagrin at your apparent indulgence of melancholy. Indeed, my friend, your own happiness and honor, require you to dissipate the cloud which hangs over your imagination.

Rise then above it; and prove yourself superior to the adverse occurrences which have befallen you. It is by surmounting difficulties, not by sinking under them, that we discover our fortitude. True courage consists not in flying from the storms of life; but in braving and steering through them with prudence. Avoid solitude. It is the bane of a disordered mind; though of great utility to a healthy one. Your once favorite amusements court your attention. Refuse not their solicitations. I have contributed my mite, by sending you a few books; such as you requested. They are of the lighter kind of reading; yet perfectly chaste; and if I mistake not, well adapted to your taste.

You wish to hear from our theatre. I believe it will be well supplied with performers this winter. Come and see whether they can afford you any entertainment. Last evening I attended a tragedy; but never will I attend another. I have not yet been able to erase the gloom which it impressed upon my mind. It was Romeo and Juliet. Distressing enough to sensibility this! Are there not real woes (if not in our own families, at least among our own

*Ultimo; of the previous month—ed.

friends, and neighbors) sufficient to exercise our sympathy and pity, without introducing fictitious ones into our very diversions? How can that be a diversion, which racks the soul with grief, even though that grief be imaginary. The introduction of a funeral solemnity, upon the stage, is shocking indeed!

Death is too serious a matter to be sported with! An opening grave cannot be a source of amusement to any considerate mind! The closing scene of life can be no pastime, when realized! it must therefore awaken painful sensations, in the representation!

The circus is a place of fashionable resort of late, but not agreeable to me. I think it inconsistent with the delicacy of a lady, even to witness the indecorums, which are practised there; especially, when the performers of equestrian feats are of our own sex. To see a woman depart so far from the female character, as to assume the masculine habit and attitudes; and appear entirely indifferent, even to the externals of modesty, is truly disgusting, and ought not to be countenanced by our attendance, much less by our approbation. But setting aside this circumstance, I cannot conceive it to be a pleasure to sit a whole evening, trembling with apprehension, lest the poor wight of a horseman, or juggler, or whatever he is to be called, should break his neck in contributing to our entertainment.

With Mr. Bowen's museum, I think you were much pleased. He has made a number of judicious additions to it, since you were here. It is a source of rational and refined amusement. Here the eye is gratified, the imagination charmed, and the understanding improved. It will bear frequent reviews without palling on the taste. It always affords something new; and for one, I am never a weary spectator.

Our other public, and private places of resort, are much as you left them.

I am happy in my present situation; but when the summer returns, I intend to visit my native home. Again, my Eliza, will we ramble together in those retired shades which friendship has ren-

dered so delightful to us. Adieu, my friend, till then. Be cheerful, and you will yet be happy.

LUCY SUMNER.

LETTER LIII.

TO MRS. LUCY SUMNER.

HARTFORD.

GRACIOUS Heaven! What have I heard? Major Sanford is married! Yes, the ungrateful, the deceitful wretch, is married! He has forsworn, he has perjured, and given himself to another! That, you will say, is nothing strange. It is characteristic of the man. It may be so; but I could not be convinced of his perfidy, till now!

Perhaps it is all for the best. Perhaps, had he remained unconnected, he might still have deceived me; but now I defy his arts!

They tell me, he has married a woman of fortune. I suppose he thinks, as I once did, that wealth can ensure happiness. I wish he may enjoy it.

This event would not affect me at all, were it not for the depression of spirits which I feel, in consequence of a previous disappointment; since which, every thing of the kind agitates and overcomes me. I will not see him. If I do, I shall betray my weakness, and flatter his vanity; as he will doubtless think he has the power of mortifying me by his connection with another.

Before this news discomposed me, I had attained to a good degree of cheerfulness. Your kind letter, seconded by Julia's exertions, had assisted me in regulating my sensibility. I have been frequently into company, and find my relish for it gradually returning.

I intend to accept the pleasure to which you invite me, of

spending a little time with you, this winter. Julia and I will come
together. Varying the scene may contribute effectually to dissi-
pate the gloom of my imagination. I would fly to almost any re-
sort, rather than my own mind. What a dreadful thing it is to be
afraid of one's own reflections, which ought to be a constant
source of enjoyment! But I will not moralize. I am sufficiently
melancholy, without any additional cause to increase it!

<div align="right">ELIZA WHARTON.</div>

LETTER LIV.

TO MR. CHARLES DEIGHTON.

<div align="right">HARTFORD.</div>

Dear Deighton,

WHO do you think is writing to you? Why, it is your old
friend, metamorphosed into *a married man!* You stare, and
can hardly credit the assertion. I cannot realize it myself; yet, I as-
sure you, Charles, it is absolutely true! Necessity, dire necessity,
forced me into this dernier resort. I told you, some time ago, it
would come to this.

I stood aloof, as long as possible; but in vain did I attempt to
shun the noose. I must either fly to this resource; or give up all
my show, equipage, and pleasure, and degenerate into a down-
right plodding money-catcher, for a subsistance. I chose the
first; and who would not? yet I feel some remorse at taking the
girl to wife, from no better motives. She is really too good for
such an imposition. But she must blame herself, if she suffer
hereafter; for she was visibly captivated by my external appear-
ance; and wanted but very little solicitation to confer herself, and
fortune on so charming a fellow. Her parents opposed her incli-
nation, for a while, because I was a stranger, and rather too gay

for their taste. But she had not been used to contradiction, and could not bear it; and therefore they ventured not to cross her. So I bore off the prize; and a prize she really is. Five thousand pounds in possession, and more in reversion, if I do not forfeit it. This will compensate for some of my past mistakes, and set matters right for the present. I think it doing much better than to have taken the little Laurence girl, I told you of, with half the sum. Besides, my Nancy is a handsomer, and more agreeable person. But that is of little consequence to me, you know. "Beauty soon grows familiar to the lover." Were I a lover, it would be of no great avail. A lover I am; yet not of my wife. The dart which I received from Miss Wharton, sticks fast in my heart; and I assure you, I could hardly persuade myself even to appear unfaithful to her. O, Eliza, accuse me not of infidelity; for your image is my constant companion! A thousand times have I cursed the unpropitious stars, which withheld from her a fortune. That would have enabled me to marry her; and with her, even wedlock would have been supportable.

I am told, that she is still single. Her sober lover never returned. Had he loved as I did, and do, he could not have been so precipitate. But these stoic souls are good for nothing, that I know of, but

> "Fix'd like a plant, to one peculiar spot,
> To draw nutrition, propagate, and rot."

I want to see Eliza, and I must see her; yet I dread an interview. I shall frankly confess my motives for marrying; and the reasons of my conduct, before I went away. I shall own that my circumstances would not allow me to possess her; and yet that I could not resign her to another.

When I make up the matter with her, I shall solicit her friendship for my wife. By this mean I may enjoy her society, at least, which will alleviate the confinement of a married state. To my spouse I must be as civil as possible. I really wish she had less merit, that I might have a plausible excuse for neglecting her.

To morrow I shall go to Mrs. Wharton's. I am very much taken

up with complimental visits, at present. What deference is always paid to equipage! They may talk of this virtue, their learning, and what not; but without either of them, I shall bear off the palm of respect from those, who have them, unadorned with gold, and its shining appendages.

Every thing hereabouts recals Eliza to my mind. I impatiently anticipate the hour, which will convey me to her presence.

<div style="text-align: right;">PETER SANFORD.</div>

LETTER LV.

TO MRS. LUCY SUMNER.

<div style="text-align: right;">HARTFORD.</div>

A NEW scene has opened upon us to day, my dear Mrs. Sumner; a visit from Major Sanford. My mamma, Miss Granby, and myself, were sitting together in the chamber. Miss Granby was entertaining us by reading aloud in Millot's elements of history, when a servant rapped at the door, and handed in the following billet.

"Will Miss Wharton condescend to converse a few moments with her once favored Sanford? He is but too sensible that he has forfeited all claim to the privilege. He therefore presumes not to request it on the score of merit, or of former acquaintance; but solicits it from her benevolence, and pity."

I read and showed it to my mamma, and Julia. What, said I, shall I do? I wish not to see him. His artifice has destroyed my peace of mind; and his presence may open the wounds which time is closing. Act, said my mamma, agreeably to the dictates of your own judgment. I see no harm in conversing with him, said Julia. Perhaps it may remove some disagreeable thoughts, which

now oppress and give you pain. And as he is no longer a candidate for your affections, added she, with a smile, it will be less hazardous than formerly. He will not have the insolence to speak; nor you the folly to hear, the language of love.

He was accordingly invited in. When I rose to go down, I hesitated, and even trembled. I fear, said I, to myself, it will be too much for me; yet why should it? Conscious innocence will support me. This he has not. When I entered the room he stepped forward to meet me. Confusion and shame were visibly depicted in his countenance. He approached me hastily; and without uttering a word, took my hand. I withdrew it. O! Miss Wharton, said he, despise me not. I am convinced that I deserve your displeasure, and disdain; but my own heart has avenged your cause. To your own heart, then, said I, I will leave you! But why do you again seek an interview with one whom you have endeavored to mislead; with one whom you have treated with unmerited neglect? Justice to myself required my appearing before you; that by confessing my faults, and obtaining your forgiveness, I might soften the reproaches of my own mind. Will you be seated, sir? said I. Will you, rejoined he, condescend to sit with me, Eliza? I will, sir, answered I. The rights of hospitality I shall not infringe. In my own house, therefore, I shall treat you with civility. Indeed, said he, you are very severe; but I have provoked all the coldness and reserve which you can inflict!

I am a married man, Eliza. So I understand, said I; and I hope you will never treat your wife with the dissimulation and falsehood, which you have exercised towards me. Would to heaven, exclaimed he, that you were my wife! I should not then fail in my love or duty as a husband! Yet she is an amiable girl; and, had I a heart to give her, I might still be happy! but that, alas! I can never recal. Why, then, said I, did you marry her? You were doubtless master of your own actions. No, said he, I was not. The embarrassed state of my affairs precluded the possibility of acting as I wished. Loving you most ardently, I was anxious to prevent your union with another, till I could so far improve my circumstances, as to secure you from poverty and want in a connection with me.

My regard was too sincere to permit me to deceive you, by a marriage which might have proved unhappy for us both. My pride forbad my telling you the motives of my delay; and I left you to see if I could place myself in a situation worthy of your acceptance. This I could not effect; and therefore have run the risk of my future happiness, by marrying a lady of affluence. This secures to me the externals of enjoyment; but my heart, I fear, will never participate* it. Yet it affords me some degree of satisfaction that I have not involved you in distress. The only alleviation of which my banishment from you is capable, is your forgiveness. In compassion, then, refuse it not! It cannot injure you! To me it will be worth millions! He wept! Yes, Lucy, this libertine; this man of pleasure and gallantry wept! I really pitied him from my heart. I forgive you, said I, and wish you happy; yet, on this condition only, that you never again pollute my ears with the recital of your infamous passion. Yes, infamous, I call it, for what softer appellation can be given to such professions from a married man? Harbor not an idea of me, in future, inconsistent with the love and fidelity which you owe your wife; much less, presume to mention it, if you wish not to be detested by me; and for ever banished from my presence. He expressed gratitude for his absolution even upon these terms; and hoped his future conduct would entitle him to my friendship and esteem. That, I replied, time only can determine.

One favor more he begged leave to solicit; which was, that I would be a neighbor to his wife. She was a stranger, he said, and would deem my society a particular privilege. This, I told him, I could not grant, at present, whatever I might do hereafter. He did not urge it any further, but inquired after my mamma, and expressed a wish to see her. I rung the bell, and ordered her and Miss Granby to be called. When they came, he was very polite to them both; and, after usual compliments, told my mamma that he was happy in having obtained my forgiveness, to which he was anxious to have her seal affixed. My daughter, said she, is the injured party; and if she be satisfied, I shall not complain. He thanked her for her condescention; informed her that he was

*Participate [in] it.—ed.

married, and requested her to visit his wife. We then conversed upon different subjects for a short time, and he took his leave. A sigh escaped him as he departed; and a gloom was visible in his countenance, which I never observed before.

I must acknowledge that this interview has given me satisfaction. I have often told you that if I married Major Sanford, it would be from a predilecton for his situation in life. How wretched must have been my lot, had I discovered, too late, that he was by no means possessed of the independence, which I fondly anticipated. I knew not my own heart, when I contemplated a connection with him. Little did I think that my regard for Mr. Boyer was so deeply rooted, as I now find it. I foolishly imagined that I could turn my affections into what channel I pleased. What then must have been my feelings, when I found myself deprived both of inward peace, and outward enjoyment! I begin now to emerge from the darkness, in which I have been long benighted! I hope the tragic comedy, in which I have acted so conspicuous a part, will come to a happy end.

Julia and I talk, now and then, of a journey to Boston. As yet I have not resolution to act with much decision upon the subject. But, wherever I am, and whatever may be my fate, I shall always be your's in truth,

ELIZA WHARTON.

LETTER LVI.

TO MRS. LUCY SUMNER.

HARTFORD.

I BEGIN to hope we shall come to rights here, by and by. Major Sanford has returned; has made us a visit; and a treaty of peace, and amity (but not of commerce,) is ratified.

Eliza appears to be rapidly returning to her former cheerfulness, if not gaity. I hope she will not diverge too far from her present sedateness and solidity; yet I am not without apprehensions of danger, on that score. One extreme commonly succeeds another. She tells me, that she assiduously cultivates her natural vivacity; that she finds her taste for company and amusements increasing; that she dreads being alone, because past scenes arise to view which vex and discompose her.

These are indications of a mind not perfectly right. I flatter myself, however, that the time is not far distant, when her passions will vibrate with regularity.

I need not repeat to you any thing relative to Major Sanford's conciliatory visit. Eliza has given you a particular, and I believe, a faithful detail. I was called down to see this wonderful man; and disliked him exceedingly. I am astonished that Eliza's penetrating eye, has not long since read his vices in his very countenance. I am told by a friend, who has visited them, that he has an agreeable wife; and I wish she may find him a husband of the same description; but I very much doubt the accomplishment of my wish. For I have no charity for these reformed rakes.

We were walking abroad the other afternoon, and met Major Sanford and lady. Eliza did not see them till they were very near us. She started, turned pale, and then colored like crimson. I cannot but think, a little envy rankled in her heart. Major Sanford very politely accosted us; and congratulated Mrs. Sanford on this opportunity of introducing her to a particular friend; presenting Eliza. She received her with an easy dignity, and bid her welcome to this part of the country. Mrs. Sanford answered her modestly; hoped for the pleasure of a further acquaintance; and urged us, as we were not far from their house, to return with them to tea. We declined; and, wishing each other a good evening, parted. Major Sanford's eyes were rivetted on Eliza, the whole time we were together; and he seemed loath to remove them, when we separated. I suspect there is some truth in his tale of love. I shall therefore discourage Eliza from associating with him under any pretext whatever. She appeared more pensive and thoughtful than com-

mon, as we returned home; and said little the rest of the evening; but next morning was as chatty as ever.

She is warm in the praises of Mrs. Sanford, thinks her an accomplished woman, and wonders that the major could suggest an idea of marrying her for her money. She intends, she says, to visit her soon; and wishes me to accompany her. This, for her own sake, I shall defer, as long as possible.

I am, &c.

JULIA GRANBY.

LETTER LVII.

TO MRS. LUCY SUMNER.

HARTFORD.

BY Julia's advice, we have neglected the repeated invitations of Major Sanford, to visit and commence neighborhood with them, till yesterday; when we received a polite billet, requesting the honor of our company to dine. My mamma declined going; but said she had no objection to our compliance with the message, if we thought proper. Julia and I accordingly went. We found a large company assembled in a spacious hall, splendidly furnished and decorated. They were all very polite and attentive to me; but none more so than Major Sanford and his lady, who jointly strove to dissipate the pensiveness of my mind, which I found it impossible to conceal. When we were summoned to dinner, the major being near me, offered his hand, and leading me into the dining room, seated me at a table furnished with all the variety which could please the eye, or regale the taste of the most luxurious epicure. The conversation turned on various subjects, literary, political, and miscellaneous. In the evening we had a ball. Major Sanford gave the hand of his

wife to a Mr. Grey, alledging that he was a stranger, and there-
fore, entitled to particular attention; and then solicited mine for
himself. I was on the point of refusing him, but recollecting that
it might have the appearance of continued resentment, contrary
to my declaration of forgiving what was past, I complied. He
was all kindness, and assiduity; the more so, I imagine, with a
view to make amends for his former ingratitude and neglect.
Tenderness is now peculiarly soothing to my wounded heart.
He took an opportunity of conversing with his wife and me to-
gether; hoped she would be honored with my friendship, and ac-
quaintance; and begged, for her sake, that I would not be a
stranger at his house. His Nancy, he said, was far removed from
her maternal friends; but I could supply their place, if I would
generously undertake the task. She joined in expressing the
same sentiments and wishes. Alas! Sir, said I, Eliza Wharton is
not now what she once was! I labor under a depression of spir-
its, which must render my company rather painful than pleasing
to my friends. The idea of what I had been, contrasted with what
I then was, touched my sensibility; and I could not restrain the
too officious tear from stealing down my cheek. He took me by
the hand, and said, you distress me, Miss Wharton, indeed, you
distress me! Happiness must, and shall attend you! Cursed be
the wretch, who could wound a heart like your's!

Julia Granby now joined us. An inquisitive concern was visi-
ble in her countenance.

I related this conversation to her, after we returned home; but
she approved it not.

She thought Major Sanford too particularly attentive to me,
considering what had previously happened. She said it would
be noticed by others, and the world would make unfavorable re-
marks upon any appearance of intimacy between us. I care not
for that, said I. It is an ill-natured, misjudging world; and I am
not obliged to sacrifice my friends to its opinion. Were Major San-
ford a single man I should avoid his society; but since he is mar-
ried; since his wife is young, beautiful and lovely, he can have
no temptation to injure me. I therefore see no evil, which can

arise from the cultivation of friendship with *her*, at least. I relish company so little, that I may surely be indulged in selecting that which is most agreeable to my taste, to prevent my becoming quite a misanthrope.

I thank you, my dear Mrs. Sumner, for your kind letter. It was a reasonable cordial to my mind; and I will endeavor to profit by your advice.

Your remarks on the public entertainments are amusing, and as far as I am a judge, perfectly just.

I think it a pity they have not female managers for the theatre. I believe it would be under much better regulations, than at present.

With cordial respects to Mr. Sumner, I subscribe myself, yours in sincerity,

<div align="right">ELIZA WHARTON.</div>

LETTER LVIII.

TO MR. CHARLES DEIGHTON.

<div align="right">HARTFORD.</div>

REJOICE with me, my friend, that I have made my peace with the mistress of my heart. No devotee could have been more sincere in his penitence, than I was in mine. Indeed, Charles, I never knew I had so much sensibility before! Why, I was as much a woman as the very weakest of the sex!

But I dealt very plainly and sincerely with her, to be sure; and this atones for all past offences, and procures absolution for many others yet to be committed.

The dear girl was not inexorable; she was as placable and condescending as I could expect, considering the nature of the crime, which was apparently slighting her person and charms,

by marrying another. This you know is one of the nicest points with the ladies. Attack their honor, that is their chastity, and they construe it to be the effect of excessive love, which hurries you a little beyond the bounds of prudence. But touch their vanity, by preferring another, and they will seldom pardon you. You will say I am very severe upon the sex. And have I not reason to be so, since I have found so many frail ones among them. This, however, is departing from my subject.

Eliza is extremely altered! Her pale dejected countenance, with the sedateness of her manners, so different from the lively glow of health, cheerfulness and activity which formerly animated her appearance and deportment, struck me very disagreeably.

With all my gallantry, and fluency in love matters, I was unable to acquit myself tolerably; or to address her with any degree of ease and confidence. She was very calm; and spoke with great indifference about my marriage, &c. which mortified me exceedingly. Yet I cannot consent to believe that her present depression of spirits arises solely from Mr. Boyer's infidelity. I flatter myself that I am of sufficient consequence to her, to have contributed in a degree.

When I inquired after her health, she told me she had been indisposed; but was now much better. This indisposition, I am informed, was purely mental; and I am happy to observe her recovering from it. I frequently visit her, sometimes with, and sometimes without my wife; of whom, through my mediation, she has become a favorite. I have married, and according to the general opinion, reformed. Yet I suspect my reformation, like most others of the kind, will prove instable as "the baseless fabric of a vision;" unless I banish myself entirely from her society. But that I can never do; for she is still lovely in my eyes, and I cannot control my passions. When absent from her, I am lost to every thing but her idea. My wife begins to rally me on my fondness for Miss Wharton. She asked me the other day if she had a fortune? No, said I, if she had I should have married her. This wounded her sensibility. I repented of my sincerity, and made

my peace for that time. Yet, I find myself growing extremely irri-
table, and she must take heed how she provokes me; for I do not
love her; and I think the name of wife becomes more and more
distasteful to me every day.

In my mind Eliza has no competitor. But I must keep up ap-
pearances, though I endeavor to regain her love. I imagine that
the enjoyment of her society, as a neighbor and friend may con-
tent me for the present, and render my condition supportable.

Farewell, Charles. I hope you will never be embarrassed with
a wife, nor lack some favorite nymph to supply the place of one.

PETER SANFORD.

LETTER LIX.

TO MRS. LUCY SUMNER.

HARTFORD.

Dear Lucy,

I INTENDED, this week, to have journeyed to Boston with Ju-
lia Granby; but my resolution fails me. I find it painful even
to think of mixing again with the gay multitude. I believe the mel-
ancholy reflections, by which I am oppressed, will be more effec-
tually, if not more easily surmounted, by tarrying where they
are rendered familiar, than by going from them awhile, and then
returning.

Julia will therefore go without me. I envy her no enjoyment
there, except your company.

The substitution of friendship in the place of love for Major
Sanford, I find productive of agreeable sensations. With him, he
assures me, it is a far more calm, and rational pleasure. *He* treats
me with the affection and tenderness of a brother; and his *wife*,
who exceeds him in professions of regard, with all the consoling

softness, and attention of a sister. Indeed, their politeness has greatly contributed to revive the cheerfulness of my natural disposition.

I believe the major's former partiality to me, as a lover, is intirely obliterated; and for my part, I feel as little restraint in his company, and his lady's, as in that of any other in the neighborhood.

I very much regret the departure of Julia; and hope you will permit her to return to me again, as soon as possible. She is a valuable friend. Her mind is well cultivated; and she has treasured up a fund of knowledge and information, which renders her company both agreeable and useful in every situation of life. We lately spent the afternoon and evening at Mr. Smith's. They had a considerable number of visitants; and among the rest, Major Sanford. His wife was expected, but did not come, being indisposed.

I believe, my friend, you must excuse me if my letters are shorter than formerly. Writing is not so agreeable to me as it used to be. I love my friends as well as ever; but I think they must be weary of the gloom and dulness which pervades my present correspondence. When my pen shall have regained its original fluency and alertness, I will resume and prolong the pleasing task.

I am, my dear Lucy, yours most affectionately,

 ELIZA WHARTON.

Letter LX.

TO THE SAME.

HARTFORD.

Dear Madam,

A GREEABLY to your desire, every art has been tried, every allurement held out, every argument used, and every plan adopted which Mrs. Wharton and I could devise to induce Eliza to accompany me to Boston; but all in vain. Sometimes she has been almost persuaded to a compliance with our united request; but soon has resolutely determined against it. I have observed her sentiments to be suddenly changed after being in company with Major Sanford. This alarms us exceedingly. Indeed the major seems to have insinuated himself into her good opinion more than ever. She is flattered into the belief that his attention to her is purely the result of friendship and benevolence.

I have not so favorable an opinion of the man, as to suppose him capable of either. He has become very familiar here. He calls in almost every day. Sometimes he but just inquires after our health; and sometimes makes long visits. The latter is his invariable practice, when he finds Eliza alone. Mrs. Wharton always avoids seeing him if she can. She dreads, she says, his approaching the house.

I entered the parlor the other day, somewhat suddenly, and found him sitting very near Eliza, in a low conversation. They both rose in apparent confusion, and he soon retired.

When he was gone; I suspect, said I, that the major was whispering a tale of love, Eliza? Do you imagine, said she, that I would listen to such a theme from a married man? I hope not, said I; but his conduct towards you indicates a revival of his former sentiments, at least. I was not aware of that, said she. As

yet I have observed nothing in his behavior to me, inconsistent with the purest friendship.

We drank tea not long since at Mr. Smith's. Late in the afternoon, Major Sanford made his appearance to apologize, as he said, for Mrs. Sanford, who was indisposed, and could not enjoy the pleasure of the visit she had contemplated. He was very gay, the whole evening; and when the company separated, he was the first to present his arm to Eliza, who accepted it without hesitation. A Mr. Newhall attended me, and we endeavored to keep them company; but they evidently chose to walk by themselves. Mr. Newhall observed, that if Major Sanford were not married, he should suspect he still intended a union with Miss Wharton. I replied, that their former intercourse having terminated in friendship, rendered them more familiar with each other, than with the generality of their acquaintance.

When we reached the house, Mr. Newhall chose not to go in, and took his leave. I waited at the door for Eliza and Major Sanford. At some little distance I saw him press her hand to his lips. It vexed me exceedingly; and no sooner had they come up, than I sullenly bade him good night, and walked directly in. Eliza soon followed me. I sat down by the fire in a thoughtful posture. She did the same. In this situation we both remained for some time, without speaking a word. At length she said, you seem not to have enjoyed your walk, Miss Granby; did you not like your gallant? Yes, said I, very well; but I am mortified that you were not better provided for. I make no complaint, rejoined she; I was very well entertained. That is what displeases me, said I; I mean your visible fondness for the society of such a man. Were you averse to it, as you ought to be, there would be no danger. But he has an alluring tongue, and a treacherous heart. How can you be pleased and entertained by his conversation? to me it appears totally repugnant to that refinement and delicacy for which you have always been esteemed.

His assiduity, and obtrusion ought to alarm you. You well know what his character has been. Marriage has not changed his

disposition. It is only a cloak which conceals it. Trust him not then, my dear Eliza! If you do, depend upon it, you will find his professions of friendship to be mere hypocricy, and deceit! I fear that he is acting over again the same unworthy arts, which formerly mislead you. Beware of his wiles! Your friends are anxious for you. They tremble at your professed regard, and apparent intimacy with that unprincipled man. My friends, said she, are very jealous of me, lately. I know not how I have forfeited their confidence, or incurred their suspicion. By encouraging that attention, I warmly replied, and receiving those caresses from a married man, which are due from him to none but his wife! He is a villian, if he deceived her into marriage by insincere professions of love. If he had then an affection for her, and has already discarded it, he is equally guilty! Can *you* expect sincerity from the man, who withholds it from an amiable, and deserving wife? No, Eliza; it is not love, which induces him to entertain you with the subject! It is a baser passion; and if you disdain not his artifice; if you listen to his flattery, you will, I fear, fall a victim to his evil machinations! If he conducted like a man of honor, he would merit your esteem; but his behavior is quite the reverse! Yet vile as he is, he would not dare to lisp his insolent hopes of your regard, if you punished his presumption with the indignation it deserves; if you spurned from your presence the ungrateful wretch, who would requite your condescension by triumphing in your ruin!

She now burst into tears, and begged me to drop the subject. Her mind, she said, was racked by her own reflections. She could bear but little. Kindness deceived, and censure distressed her!

I assured her of my good intentions; that as I saw her danger, I thought it a duty of the friendship and affection I bore her, solemnly to warn her against it before we parted. We talked over the matter more calmly, till she professed herself resolved in future to avoid his company, and reject his insinuations.

The next day, as I walked out, I met Major Sanford. He ac-

costed me very civilly. I barely bid him good morning, and passed on.

I made it in my way to call at his house, and bid Mrs. Sanford adieu; not expecting another opportunity equally favorable. When I entered the parlor, she was playing a melancholy air on the harpsicord. She rose, and gave me a polite and graceful reception. I told her, as I was soon to leave town, I called to take my leave of her; a compliment, which her attention to me required. Are you going to leave us then, Miss Granby? said she. I shall regret your departure exceedingly. I have so few friends in this part of the country, that it will give me sensible pain to part with one I so highly value.

I told her in the course of conversation, that I expected the pleasure of seeing her yesterday at Mr. Smith's; and was very sorry for the indisposition, which prevented her favoring us with her company. Indeed, said she, I did not know I was expected there! Were you there pray? Yes, said I; and Major Sanford excused your not coming, on the account I have mentioned. Well, said she, this is the first word I ever heard about it; he told me that business led him abroad! Did he gallant any lady? O, said I, he was with us all together. We had no particular gallants.

Seeing her curiosity excited, I heartily repented saying any thing of the matter, and waved the subject. Little did I suspect him to have been guilty of so base an artifice! It was evidently contrived to facilitate an interview with Eliza.

When I returned I related this affair to Mrs. Wharton and her daughter. The old lady and I expatiated largely on the vileness of this conduct; and endeavored to expose it to Eliza's view in its true colors. She pretended not to justify it. Yet she looked as if she wished it in her power.

I am now preparing for my journey to Boston; which I must however defer another week, for the sake of a more agreeable passage in the stage. I regret leaving Eliza! I tremble at her danger! She has not the resolution to resist temptation, which she once possessed. Her mind is surprisingly weakened! She ap-

pears sensible of this; yet adds to it by yielding to her own imbe-
cility. You will receive a letter from her with this; though I had
much difficulty to persuade her to write. She has unfortunately
become very averse to this, her once favorite amusement.

As I shall soon have the pleasure of conversing with you per-
sonally, I conclude without any other addition to this scroll, than
the name of your obliged

<div align="right">JULIA GRANBY.</div>

LETTER LXI.

TO MISS ELIZA WHARTON.

<div align="right">BOSTON.</div>

My Dear Friend,

I HAVE received your letters, and must own to you that the pe-
rusal of them gave me pain. Pardon my suspicions, Eliza:
they are excited by real friendship. Julia, you say, approves not
Major Sanford's particular attention to you. Neither do I. If you
recollect, and examine his conversation in his conciliatory visit,
you will find it replete with sentiments, for the avowal of which,
he ought to be banished from all virtuous society.

Does he not insidiously declare that you are the only object of
his affections; that his union with another was formed from inter-
ested views; and though that other is acknowledged to be amia-
ble and excellent, still he has not a heart to bestow, and expects
not happiness with her? Does this discover even the appearance
of amendment? Has he not, by false pretensions, mislead a virtu-
ous woman, and induced her to form a connection with him?
She was a stranger to his manner of life; and doubtless allured,
as you have been, by flattery, deceit, and external appearance,

to trust his honor; little thinking him wholly devoid of that sacred tie! What is the reward of her confidence? Insensibility to her charms, neglect of her person, and professed attachment to another!

Is he the man, my dear Eliza, whose friendship you wish to cultivate? Can that heavenly passion reside in a breast, which is the seat of treachery, duplicity, and ingratitude? You are too sensible of its purity and worth, to suppose it possible. The confessions of his own mouth condemn him. They convince me that he is still the abandoned libertine; and that marriage is but the cloak of his intrigues. His officious attentions to you are alarming to your friends. You own your mind weakened, and peculiarly susceptible of tender impressions. Beware how you receive them from him. Listen not a moment to his flattering professions. It is an insult upon your understanding for him to offer them. It is derogatory to virtue for you to hear them.

Slight not the opinion of the world. We are dependent beings; and while the smallest traces of virtuous sensibility remain, we must feel the force of that dependence, in a greater or less degree. No female, whose mind is uncorrupted, can be indifferent to reputation. It is an inestimable jewel, the loss of which can never be repaired. While retained, it affords conscious peace to our own minds, and ensures the esteem and respect of all around us.

Blessed with the company of so disinterested and faithful a friend, as Julia Granby, some deference is certainly due to her opinion and advice. To an enlarged understanding, a cultivated taste, and an extensive knowledge of the world, she unites the most liberal sentiments, with a benevolence, and candor of disposition, which render her equally deserving of your confidence and affection.

I cannot relinquish my claim to a visit from you this winter. Marriage has not alieniated, or weakened my regard for my friends. Come, then, to your faithful Lucy. Have you sorrows? I will sooth, and alleviate them. Have you cares? I will dispel

them. Have you pleasures? I will heighten them. Come then, let me fold you to my expecting heart. My happiness will be partly suspended till your society render it complete. Adieu.

LUCY SUMNER.

LETTER LXII.

TO MISS JULIA GRANBY.

HARTFORD.

Dear Julia,

I HOPE Mrs. Sumner and you will excuse my writing but one letter, in answer to the number I have received from you both. Writing is an employment, which suits me not at present. It was pleasing to me formerly, and therefore, by recalling the idea of circumstances and events which frequently occupied my pen in happier days, it now gives me pain. Yet I have just written a long consolatory letter to Mrs. Richman. She has buried her babe; her little Harriot, of whom she was doatingly fond.

It was a custom with some of the ancients, we are told, to weep at the birth of their children.

Often should we be impelled to a compliance with this custom, could we foresee the future incidents of their lives. I think, at least, that the uncertainty of their conduct and condition in more advanced age, may reconcile us to their removal to a happier state, before they are capable of tasting the bitterness of woe.

> "Happy the babe, who, priviledg'd by fate,
> To shorter labors, and a lighter weight,
> Receiv'd but yesterday the gift of breath;
> Order'd to morrow, to return to death."

Our domestic affairs are much as when you left us. Nothing remarkable has occurred in the neighborhood, worth communicating. The company and amusements of the town are as usual, I suppose. I frequent neither of them. Having incurred so much censure by the indulgence of a gay disposition, I am now trying what a recluse and solitary mode of life will produce. You will call me splenetic. I own it. I am pleased with nobody; still less with myself. I look around for happiness, and find it not. The world is to me a desart*! If I indulge myself in temporary enjoyment, the consciousness or apprehension of doing amiss, destroys my peace of mind. And, when I have recourse to books, if I read those of serious description, they remind me of an awful futurity, for which I am unprepared; if history, it discloses facts in which I have no interest; if novels, they exhibit scenes of pleasure which I have no prospect of realizing!

My mamma is solicitously attentive to my happiness; and though she fails of promoting it; yet I endeavor to save her the pangs of disappointment, by appearing what she wishes.

I anticipate, and yet I dread your return; a paradox this, which time alone can solve.

Continue writing to me, and intreat Mrs. Sumner, in my name, to do likewise. Your benevolence must be your reward.

ELIZA WHARTON.

*Desert—ed.

Letter LXIII.

TO MISS ELIZA WHARTON.

BOSTON.

A PARADOX, indeed, is the greater part of your letter to us, my dear Eliza. We had fondly flattered ourselves that the melancholy of your mind was exterminated. I hope no new cause has revived it. Little did I intend, when I left you, to have been absent so long; but Mrs. Sumner's disappointment, in her plan of spending the summer at Hartford, induced me, in compliance with her request, to prolong my residence here.

But for your sake, she now consents to my leaving her, in hopes I may be so happy as to contribute to your amusement.

I am both pleased and instructed by the conduct of this amiable woman. As I always endeavored to imitate her discreet and modest behavior in a single state; so likewise shall I take her for a pattern, should I ever enter a married life. She is most happily united. Mr. Sumner, to all the graces and accomplishments of the gentleman, adds the still more important and essential properties of virtue, integrity and honor. I was once present when a person was recommended to her for a husband. She objected that he was a rake. True, said the other, he has been, but he has reformed. That will never do for me, rejoined she; I wish my future companion to need no reformation: a sentiment worthy the attention of our whole sex; the general adoption of which, I am persuaded, would have a happy influence upon the manners of the other.

I hope neither you, nor I, Eliza, shall ever be tried by a man of debauched principles. Such characters I conceive to be totally unfit for the society of women, who have any claim to virtue and delicacy.

I intend to be with you, in about a month. If agreeable to you,

we will visit, and spend a few weeks with the afflicted Mrs. Rich-
man. I sincerely sympathize with her, under her bereavement. I
know her fondness for you will render your company very con-
soling to her; and I flatter myself that I should not be an unwel-
come guest.

Make my respects to your mamma; and believe me ever yours,

JULIA GRANBY.

LETTER LXIV.

TO MRS. LUCY SUMNER.

HARTFORD.

Dear Madam,

I HAVE arrived in safety, to the mansion of our once happy
and social friends. But I cannot describe to you, how
changed, how greatly changed this amiable family appears since
I left it. Mrs. Wharton met me at the door; and tenderly embrac-
ing, bade me a cordial welcome. You are come, Julia, said she, I
hope, to revive and comfort us. We have been very solitary dur-
ing your absence. I am happy madam, said I, to return; and my
endeavors to restore cheerfulness and content, shall not be want-
ing. But, where is Eliza? By this time we had reached the back
parlor, whither Mrs. Wharton led me; and the door being open,
I saw Eliza, reclined on a settee, in a very thoughtful posture.
When I advanced to meet her, she never moved; but sat "like pa-
tience on a monument, smiling at grief!"

I stopped involuntarily, and involuntarily raising my eyes to
heaven, exclaimed, is that Eliza Wharton! She burst into tears;
and attempted to rise, but sunk again into her seat. Seeing her
thus affected, I sat down by her; and throwing my arm about her
neck, why these tears? said I. Why this distress, my dear friend?

Let not the return of your Julia give you pain! She comes to sooth you with the consolations of friendship! It is not pain, said she, clasping me to her breast; it is pleasure, too exquisite for my weak nerves to bear! See you not, Julia, how I am altered? Should you have known me for the sprightly girl, who was always welcome at the haunts of hilarity and mirth? Indeed, said I, you appear indisposed, but I will be your physician. Company, and change of air will, I doubt not, restore you. Will these cure disorders of the mind, Julia? They will have a powerful tendency to remove them, if rightly applied; and I profess considerable skill in that art. Come, continued I, we will try these medicines in the morning. Let us rise early, and step into the chaise; and after riding a few miles, call and breakfast with Mrs. Freeman. I have some commissions from her daughter. We shall be agreeably entertained there, you know.

Being summoned to supper, I took her by the hand, and we walked into another room, where we found her brother, and his wife, with her mamma waiting for us. We were all very chatty; even Eliza resumed, in a degree, her former sociability. A settled gloom, notwithstanding, brooded on her countenance; and a deep sigh often escaped her, in spite of her evident endeavors to suppress it. She went to bed before us; when her mamma informed me that her health had been declining for some months, that she never complained, but studiously concealed every symptom of indisposition. Whether it were any real disorder of body, or whether it arose from her depression of spirits, she could not tell; but supposed they operated together, and mutually heightened each other.

I inquired after Major Sanford; whether he and Eliza had associated together during my absence? Sometimes, she said, they seemed on good terms; and he frequently called to see her; at others, they had very little, if any correspondence at all. She told me that Eliza never went abroad, and was very loath to see company at home; that her chief amusement consisted in solitary walks; that the dreadful idea of her meeting Major Sanford in these walks, had now and then intruded upon her imagination;

that she had not the least evidence of the fact, however; and indeed, was afraid to make any inquiries into the matter, lest her own suspicions should be discovered; that the major's character was worse than ever; that he was much abroad, and frequently entertained large parties of worthless bacchanalians at his house; that common report said he treated his wife with indifference, neglect, and ill nature; with many other circumstances, which it is not material to relate.

Adieu, my dear friend, for the present. When occasion requires, you shall hear again from your affectionate

<div align="right">JULIA GRANBY.</div>

LETTER LXV.

TO MR. CHARLES DEIGHTON.

<div align="right">HARTFORD.</div>

GOOD news, Charles, good news! I have arrived to the utmost bounds of my wishes; the full possession of my adorable Eliza! I have heard a quotation from a certain book; but what book it was I have forgotten, if I ever knew. No matter for that; the quotation is, that "stolen waters are sweet, and bread eaten in secret is pleasant." If it has reference to the pleasures, which I have enjoyed with Eliza, I like it hugely, as Tristram Shandy's father said of Yorick's sermon; and I think it fully verified.

I had a long and tedious siege. Every method which love could suggest, or art invent, was adopted. I was sometimes ready to despair, under an idea that her resolution was unconquerable, her virtue impregnable. Indeed, I should have given over the pursuit long ago, but for the hopes of success I entertained from her parleying with me, and in reliance upon her own strength, endeavoring to combat, and counteract my de-

signs. Whenever this has been the case, Charles, I have never yet been defeated in my plan. If a lady will consent to enter the lists against the antagonist of her honor, she may be sure of losing the prize. Besides, were her delicacy genuine, she would banish the man at once, who presumed to doubt, which he certainly does, who attempts to vanquish it!

But, far be it from me to criticise the pretensions of the sex. If I gain the rich reward of my dissimulation and gallantry, that you know is all I want.

To return then to the point. An unlucky, but not a miraculous accident, has taken place, which must soon expose our amour. What can be done? At the first discovery, absolute distraction seized the soul of Eliza, which has since terminated in a fixed melancholy. Her health too is much impaired. She thinks herself rapidly declining; and I tremble when I see her emaciated form!

My wife has been reduced very low, of late. She brought me a boy a few weeks past, a dead one though.

These circumstances give me neither pain nor pleasure. I am too much ingrossed by my divinity, to take an interest in any thing else. True, I have lately suffered myself to be somewhat engaged here and there by a few jovial lads, who assist me in dispelling the anxious thoughts, which my perplexed situation excites. I must, however, seek some means to relieve Eliza's distress. My finances are low; but the last fraction shall be expended in her service, if she need it.

Julia Granby is expected at Mrs. Wharton's every hour. I fear that her inquisitorial eye will soon detect our intrigue, and obstruct its continuation. Now there's a girl, Charles, I should never attempt to seduce; yet she is a most alluring object, I assure you. But the dignity of her manners forbid all assaults upon her virtue. Why, the very expression of her eye, blasts in the bud, every thought, derogatory to her honor; and tells you plainly, that the first insinuation of the kind, would be punished with eternal banishment and displeasure! Of her there is no danger! But I can write no more, except that I am, &c.

PETER SANFORD.

LETTER LXVI.

TO MRS. LUCY SUMNER.

HARTFORD.

O H, my friend! I have a tale to unfold; a tale which will rend every nerve of sympathizing pity, which will rack the breast of sensibility, and unspeakably distress your benevolent heart! Eliza—Oh the ruined, lost Eliza!

I want words to express the emotions of indignation, and grief which oppress me! But I will endeavor to compose myself; and relate the circumstances as they came to my knowledge.

After my last letter, Eliza remained much in the same gloomy situation as I found her. She refused to go, agreeably to her promise, to visit your mamma; and under one pretext or another, has constantly declined accompanying me any where else, since my arrival.

Till last Thursday night she slept in the same bed with me; when she excused herself, by saying she was restless, and should disturb my repose. I yielded to her humor of taking a different apartment, little suspecting the real cause! She frequently walked out; and though I sometimes followed, I very seldom found her. Two or three times, when I happened to be awake, I heard her go down stairs; and on inquiry in the morning, she told me that she was very thirsty, and went down for water. I observed a degree of hesitancy in her answers, for which I could not account. But last night, the dreadful mystery was developed! A little before day, I heard the front door opened with great caution. I sprang from my bed, and running to the window, saw by the light of the moon, a man going from the house. Soon after I perceived a footstep upon the stairs, which carefully approached and entered Eliza's chamber.

Judge of my astonishment, my surprise, my feelings, upon

this occasion! I doubted not but Major Sanford was the person I had seen; and the discovery of Eliza's guilt, in this infamous intrigue, almost deprived me of thought and recollection! My blood thrilled with horror at this sacrifice of virtue! After a while I recovered myself, and put on my clothes. But what to do, I knew not; whether to go directly to her chamber, and let her know that she was detected; or to wait another opportunity.

I resolved on the first. The day had now dawned. I tapped at her door; and she bid me come in. She was sitting in an easy chair by the side of her bed. As I entered she withdrew her handkerchief from her face; and looking earnestly at me, said, what procures me the favor of a visit, at this early hour, Miss Granby? I was disturbed, said I, and wished not to return to my bed. But what breaks your rest; and calls you up so unseasonably, Eliza? Remorse, and despair, answered she, weeping. After what I have witnessed, this morning, rejoined I, I cannot wonder at it! Was it not Major Sanford whom I saw go from the house some time ago? She was silent, but tears flowed abundantly. It is too late, continued I, to deny, or evade. Answer my question sincerely; for, believe me, Eliza, it is not malice, but concern for you, which prompts it. I will answer you, Julia, said she. You have discovered a secret, which harrows up my very soul! A secret, which I wished you to know, but could not exert resolution to reveal! Yes! It was Major Sanford; the man who has robbed me of my peace; who has triumphed in my destruction; and who will cause my sun to sit at noon!

I shudder, said I, at your confession! Wretched, deluded girl! Is this a return for your parent's love, and assiduous care; for your friends' solicitude, and premonitory advice? You are ruined, you say! You have sacrificed your virtue to an abandoned, despicable profligate! And you live to acknowledge and bear your infamy! I do, said she; but not long shall I support this burden! See you not, Julia, my decaying frame, my faded cheek, and tottering limbs? Soon shall I be insensible to censure and reproach! Soon shall I be sequestered in that mansion, "where the wicked cease from troubling, and where the weary are at rest!"

Rest! said I, can you expect to find rest either in this world, or another, with such a weight of guilt on your head? She exclaimed, with great emotion, add not to the upbraidings of a wounded spirit! Have pity upon me, Oh! my friend, have pity upon me!

Could you know what I suffer, you would think me sufficiently punished! I wish you no other punishment, said I, than what may effect your repentance and reformation. But your mother, Eliza! She cannot long be ignorant of your fall; and I tremble to think of her distress! It will break her widowed heart! How has she loved; how has she doated upon you! Dreadful is the requital which you have made! My mother, rejoined she—Oh, name her not! The very sound is distraction to me! Oh! my Julia, if your heart be not shut against mercy and compassion towards me, aid me through this trying scene! Let my situation call forth your pity, and induce you, undeserving as I am, to exert it in my behalf!

During this time, I had walked the chamber. My spirits had been raised above their natural key, and were exhausted. I sat down, but thought I should have fainted, till a copious flood of tears gave me relief. Eliza was extremely affected. The appearance of calamity which she exhibited would have softened the most obdurate anger. Indeed, I feared some immediate and fatal effect. I therefore seated myself beside her; and assuming an air of kindness, compose yourself, Eliza, said I; I repeat what I told you before, it is the purest friendship, which thus interests me in your concerns. This, under the direction of charity, induces me again to offer you my hand. Yet you have erred against knowledge and reason; against warning and counsel. You have forfeited the favor of your friends; and reluctant will be their forgiveness. I plead guilty, said she, to all your charges. From the general voice I expect no clemency. If I can make my peace with my mother, it is all I seek or wish on this side the grave.

In your benevolence I confide for this. In you, I hope to find an intercessor. By the remembrance of our former affection and happiness, I conjure you, refuse me not. At present, I entreat you to conceal from her this distressing tale. A short reprieve is

all I ask. Why, said I, should you defer it? When the painful task is over, you may find relief in her lenient kindness. After she knows my condition, I cannot see her, resumed she, till I am assured of her forgiveness. I have not strength to support the appearance of her anger and grief. I will write to her what I cannot speak. You must bear the melancholy message, and plead for me, that her displeasure may not follow me to the grave; whither I am rapidly hastening. Be assured, replied I, that I will keep your secret as long as prudence requires. But I must leave you now: your mamma will wonder at our being thus closetted together. When opportunity presents, we will converse further on the subject. In the mean time, keep yourself as composed as possible, if you would avoid suspicion. She raised her clasped hands, and with a piteous look, threw her handkerchief over her face, and reclined in her chair, without speaking a word. I returned to my chamber, and endeavored to dissipate every idea which might tend to disorder my countenance, and break the silence I wished to observe, relative to what had happened.

When I went down, Mrs. Wharton desired me to step up, and inform Eliza that breakfast was ready. She told me she could not yet compose herself sufficiently to see her mamma; and begged me to excuse her absence as I thought proper. I accordingly returned for answer to Mrs. Wharton, that Eliza had rested but indifferently, and being somewhat indisposed, would not come down, but wished me to bring her a bowl of chocolate, when we had breakfasted. I was obliged studiously to suppress even my thoughts concerning her, lest the emotions they excited might be observed. Mrs. Wharton conversed much of her daughter, and expressed great concern about her health and state of mind. Her return to this state of dejection, after having recovered her spirits and cheerfulness, in a great degree, was owing, she feared, to some cause unknown to her; and she entreated me to extract the secret, if possible. I assured her of my best endeavors, and doubted not, I told her, but I should be able in a few days to effect what she wished.

Eliza came down and walked in the garden before dinner; at

which she commanded herself much better than I expected. She said that a little ride might, she imagined, be of service to her; and asked me if I would accompany her a few miles in the afternoon. Her mamma was much pleased with the proposition; and the chaise was accordingly ordered.

I observed to Eliza, as we rode, that with her natural and acquired abilities, with her advantages of education, with her opportunities of knowing the world, and of tracing the virtues and vices of mankind to their origin, I was surprised at her becoming the prey of an insidious libertine, with whose character she was well acquainted, and whose principles she was fully apprised would prompt him to deceive and betray her. Your surprise is very natural, said she. The same will doubtless be felt and expressed by every one to whom my sad story is related. But the cause may be found in that unrestrained levity of disposition, that fondness for dissipation and coquetry which alienated the affections of Mr. Boyer from me. This event fatally depressed, and enfeebled my mind. I embraced with avidity the consoling power of friendship, ensnaringly offered by my seducer; vainly inferring from his marriage with a virtuous woman, that he had seen the error of his ways, and forsaken his licentious practices, as he affirmed, and I, fool that I was, believed it!

It is needless for me to rehearse the perfidious arts, by which he insinuated himself into my affections, and gained my confidence. Suffice it to say, he effected his purpose! But not long did I continue in the delusive dream of sensual gratification. I soon awoke to a most poignant sense of his baseness, and of my own crime and misery. I would have fled from him; I would have renounced him for ever; and by a life of sincere humility and repentance, endeavored to make my peace with heaven, and to obliterate, by the rectitude of my future conduct, the guilt I had incurred; but I found it too late! My circumstances called for attention; and I had no one to participate my cares, to witness my distress, and to alleviate my sorrows, but him. I could not therefore prevail on myself, wholly to renounce his society. At times I have admitted his visits; always meeting him in the garden, or

grove adjoining; till of late, the weather, and my ill health in-
duced me to comply with his solicitations, and receive him into
the parlor.

Not long, however, shall I be subject to these embarrass-
ments. Grief has undermined my constitution. My health has
fallen a sacrifice to a disordered mind. But I regret not its depar-
ture! I have not a single wish to live. Nothing which the world af-
fords can restore my former serenity and happiness!

The little innocent I bear, will quickly disclose its mother's
shame! God Almighty grant it may not live as a monument of
my guilt, and a partaker of the infamy and sorrow, which is all I
have to bequeath it! Should it be continued in life, it will never
know the tenderness of a parent; and, perhaps, want and dis-
grace may be its wretched portion! The greatest consolation I can
have, will be to carry it with me to a state of eternal rest; which,
vile as I am, I hope to obtain, through the infinite mercy of
heaven, as revealed in the gospel of Christ.

I must see Major Sanford again. It is necessary to converse fur-
ther with him, in order to carry my plan of operation into execu-
tion. What is this plan of operation, Eliza? said I. I am on the
rack of anxiety for your safety. Be patient, continued she, and
you shall soon be informed. To morrow I shall write my dreadful
story to my mother. She will be acquainted with my future inten-
tions; and you shall know, at the same time, the destination of
your lost friend. I hope, said I, that you have formed no resolu-
tion against your own life. God forbid, rejoined she. My breath
is in his hands, let him do what seemeth good in his sight! Keep
my secret one day longer, and I will never more impose so pain-
ful a silence upon you.

By this time we had reached home. She drank tea with compo-
sure, and soon retired to rest. Mrs. Wharton eagerly inquired
whether I had found out the cause of Eliza's melancholy. I have
urged her, said I, on the subject; but she alledges that she has
particular reasons for present concealment. She has, notwith-
standing, promised to let me know, the day after to morrow.

Oh, said she, I shall not rest till the period arrives. Dear, good woman, said I to myself, I fear you will never rest afterwards!

This is our present situation. Think what a scene rises to the view of your Julia! She must share the distresses of others, though her own feelings, on this unhappy occasion, are too keen to admit a moment's serenity! My greatest relief is in writing to you; which I shall do again by the next post. In the mean time, I must beg leave to subscribe myself, sincerely yours,

JULIA GRANBY.

LETTER LXVII.

TO THE SAME.

ALL is now lost; lost, indeed! She is gone! Yes, my dear friend, our beloved Eliza, is gone! Never more shall we behold this once amiable companion, this once innocent and happy girl. She has forsaken, and, as she says, bid an everlasting adieu to her home, her afflicted parent and her friends! But I will take up my melancholy story where I left it in my last.

She went, as she told me she expected, into the garden, and met her detestable paramour. In about an hour she returned, and went directly to her chamber. At one o'clock I went up, and found her writing, and weeping. I begged her to compose herself, and go down to dinner. No; she said, she could not eat; and was not fit to appear before any body. I remonstrated against her immoderate grief; represented the injury she must sustain by the indulgence of it, and conjured her to suppress the violence of its emotions.

She entreated me to excuse her to her mamma; said she was

writing to her, and found it a task too painful to be performed with any degree of composure; that she was almost ready to sink under the weight of her affliction; but hoped and prayed for support, both in this, and another trying scene, which awaited her. In compliance with her desire, I now left her; and told her mamma that she was very busy in writing; wished not to be interrupted at present; but would take some refreshment, an hour or two hence. I visited her again, about four o'clock; when she appeared more calm and tranquil.

It is finished, said she, as I entered her apartment, it is finished. What said I, is finished? No matter, replied she; you will know all to morrow, Julia. She complained of excessive fatigue, and expressed an inclination to lie down; in which I assisted her, and then retired. Some time after her mamma went up, and found her still on the bed. She rose, however, and accompanied her down stairs. I met her at the door of the parlor, and taking her by the hand, inquired how she did? Oh, Julia, miserably indeed, said she. How severely does my mother's kindness reproach me! How insupportably it increases my self-condemnation! She wept; she wrung her hands, and walked the room in the greatest agony! Mrs. Wharton was exceedingly distressed by her appearance. Tell me, Eliza, said she, tell me the cause of your trouble! Oh, kill me not by your mysterious concealment! My dear child, let me, by sharing, alleviate your affliction! Ask me not, madam, said she; O my mother, I conjure you not to insist on my divulging to night, the fatal secret which engrosses and distracts my mind! To morrow I will hide nothing from you. I will press you no further, rejoined her mamma. Chuse your own time, my dear; but remember, I must participate* your grief, though I know not the cause.

Supper was brought in; and we endeavored to prevail on Eliza to eat, but in vain. She sat down, in compliance with our united importunities; but neither of us tasted food. It was removed untouched. For a while, Mrs. Wharton and I gazed in silent anguish upon the spectacle of woe, before us! At length, Eliza rose

*Participate [in] your grief—ed.

to retire. Julia, said she, will you call at my chamber, as you pass to your own? I assented. She then approached her mamma, fell upon her knees before her, and clasping her hand, said, in broken accents, Oh madam! can you forgive a wretch, who has forfeited your love, your kindness, and your compassion? Surely, Eliza, said she, you are not that being! No, it is impossible! But however great your transgression, be assured of my forgiveness, my compassion, and my continued love! Saying this, she threw her arms about her daughter's neck, and affectionately kissed her. Eliza struggled from her embrace, and looking at her with wild despair, exclaimed, this is too much! Oh, this unmerited goodness is more than I can bear! She then rushed precipitately out of the room, and left us overwhelmed in sympathy and astonishment!

When Mrs. Wharton had recovered herself a little, she observed, that Eliza's brain was evidently disordered. Nothing else, continued she, could impel her to act in this extraordinary manner. At first she was resolved to follow her; but I dissuaded her from it, alledging, that as she had desired me to come into her chamber, I thought it better for me to go alone. She acquiesced; but said she should not think of going to bed; but would, however, retire to her chamber, and seek consolation there. I bade her good night; and went up to Eliza, who took me by the hand and led me to the toilet, upon which she laid the two inclosed letters, the one to her mamma, and the other to me. These, said she, contain what I had not resolution to express. Promise me, Julia, that they shall not be opened till to morrow morning. I will, said I. I have thought and wept, continued she, till I have almost exhausted my strength, and my reason. I would now obtain a little respite, that I may prepare my mind for the account I am one day to give at a higher tribunal than that of earthly friends. For this purpose, what I have written, and what I shall yet say to you, must close the account between you and me. I have certainly no balance against you, said I. In my breast you are fully acquitted. Your penitential tears have obliterated your guilt, and blotted out your errors with your Julia.

Henceforth, be they all forgotten. Live, and be happy. Talk not, said she, of life. It would be a vain hope, though I cherished it myself.

> "That I must die, it is my only comfort;
> Death is the privilege of human nature;
> And life without it were not worth our taking.
> Thither the poor, the prisoner and the mourner
> Fly for relief, and lay their burdens down!"

You have forgiven me, Julia; my mother has assured me of her forgiveness, and what have I more to wish? My heart is much lightened by these kind assurances; they will be a great support to me in the dreadful hour which awaits me! What mean you, Eliza? said I. I fear some desperate purpose labors in your mind. Oh, no, she replied; you may be assured your fear is groundless. I know not what I say; my brain is on fire; I am all confusion! Leave me, Julia; when I have had a little rest, I shall be composed. These letters have almost distracted me; but they are written, and I am comparatively easy. I will not leave you, Eliza, said I, unless you will go directly to bed, and endeavor to rest. I will, said she, and the sooner the better. I tenderly embraced her, and retired, though not to bed. About an hour after, I returned to her chamber, and opening the door very softly, found her apparently asleep. I acquainted Mrs. Wharton with her situation, which was a great consolation to us both; and encouraged us to go to bed. Having suffered much in my mind, and being much fatigued, I soon fell asleep; but the rattling of a carriage, which appeared to stop at a little distance from the house, awoke me. I listened a moment, and heard the door turn slowly on its hinges. I sprang from my bed, and reached the window just in time to see a female handed into a chaise by a man who hastily followed her, and drove furiously away! I at once concluded they could be no other than Eliza and Major Sanford. Under this impression I made no delay, but ran immediately to her chamber. A candle was burning on the table; but Eliza was not there! I thought it best to acquaint her mamma with the melancholy dis-

covery; and steping to her apartment for the purpose, found her rising. She had heard me walk, and was anxious to know the cause. What is the matter, Julia, said she; what is the matter? Dear madam, said I, arm yourself with fortitude! What new occurrence demands it? rejoined she. Eliza has left us! Left us! what mean you? She is just gone! I saw her handed into a chaise, which instantly disappeared!

At this intelligence she gave a shriek, and fell back on her bed! I alarmed the family, and by their assistance soon recovered her. She desired me to inform her of every particular relative to her elopement, which I did; and then delivered her the letter which Eliza had left for her. I suspect, said she, as she took it; I have long suspected, what I dared not believe! The anguish of my mind has been known only to myself, and my God! I could not answer her, and therefore withdrew. When I had read Eliza's letter to me, and wept over the sad fall; and, as I fear, the total loss of this once amiable and accomplished girl, I returned to Mrs. Wharton. She was sitting in her easy chair; and still held the fatal letter in her hand. When I entered, she fixed her streaming eyes upon me, and exclaimed, O Julia, this is more than the bitterness of death! True, madam, said I, your affliction must be great; yet that all-gracious Being, who controls every event, is able, and I trust, disposed to support you! To Him, replied she, I desire humbly to resign myself; but I think I could have borne almost any other calamity with greater resignation and composure than this. With how much comparative ease could I have followed her to the grave, at any period since her birth! Oh, my child, my child! dear, very dear hast thou been to my fond heart! Little did I think it possible for you to prepare so dreadful a cup of sorrow for your widowed mother! But where, continued she, where can the poor fugitive have fled? Where can she find that protection and tenderness, which, notwithstanding her great apostacy, I should never have withheld? From whom can she receive those kind attentions, which her situation demands.

The agitation of her mind had exhausted her strength; and I prevailed on her to refresh, and endeavor to compose herself to

rest; assuring her of my utmost exertions to find out Eliza's re-
treat, and restore her to a mother's arms.

I am obliged to suppress my own emotions; and to bend all
my thoughts towards the alleviation of Mrs. Wharton's anxiety
and grief.

Major Sanford is from home, as I expected; and I am deter-
mined, if he return, to see him myself, and extort from him the
place of Eliza's concealment. Her flight, in her present state of
health, is inexpressibly distressing to her mother; and, unless
we find her soon, I dread the effects!

I shall not close this, till I have seen or heard from the vile mis-
creant who has involved a worthy family in wretchedness!

Friday Morning—Two days have elapsed without affording us
much relief. Last evening, I was told that Major Sanford was at
home. I immediately wrote him a billet, entreating and conjur-
ing him to let me know where the hapless Eliza had fled. He re-
turned me the following answer.

"Miss Granby need be under no apprehensions, respecting
the situation of our beloved Eliza. She is well provided for, con-
veniently accommodated, and has every thing to make her
happy, which love or affluence can give.

Major Sanford has solemnly sworn not to discover her retreat.
She wishes to avoid the accusations of her friends, till she is bet-
ter able to bear them.

Her mother may rest assured of immediate information,
should any danger threaten her amiable daughter; and also of
having seasonable notice of her safety."

Although little dependence can be placed upon this man; yet
these assurances have, in a great degree, calmed our minds. We
are, however, contriving means to explore the refuge of the wan-
derer; and hope, by tracing his steps, to accomplish our pur-
pose. This we have engaged a friend to do.

I know, my dear Mrs. Sumner, the kind interest you will take
in this disastrous affair. I tremble to think what the event may
be! To relieve your suspense, however, I shall write you every
circumstance, as it occurs. But at present, I shall only enclose

Eliza's letters to her mamma, and me, and, subscribe myself
your sincere and obliged friend,

JULIA GRANBY.

LETTER LXVIII.

TO MRS. M. WHARTON.

TUESDAY.

My Honored And Dear Mamma,

IN what words, in what language shall I address you? What
shall I say on a subject which deprives me of the power of ex-
pression? Would to God I had been totally deprived of that
power before so fatal a subject required its exertion! Repentance
comes too late, when it cannot prevent the evil lamented. For
your kindness, your more than maternal affection towards me,
from my infancy to the present moment, a long life of filial duty
and unerring rectitude could hardly compensate. How greatly
deficient in gratitude must I appear then, while I confess, that
precept and example, counsel and advice, instruction and admo-
nition, have been all lost upon me!

Your kind endeavors to promote my happiness have been re-
paid by the inexcusable folly of sacrificing it. The various emo-
tions of shame, and remorse, penitence and regret, which tor-
ture and distract my guilty breast, exceed description. Yes,
madam, your Eliza has fallen; fallen, indeed! She has become the
victim of her own indiscretion, and of the intrigue and artifice of
a designing libertine, who is the husband of another! She is pol-
luted, and no more worthy of her parentage! She flies from you,
not to conceal her guilt, that she humbly and penitently owns;
but to avoid what she has never experienced, and feels herself
unable to support, a mother's frown; to escape the heart-rending

sight of a parent's grief, occasioned by the crimes of her guilty child!

I have become a reproach and disgrace to my friends. The consciousness of having forfeited their favor, and incurred their disapprobation and resentment, induces me to conceal from them the place of my retirement; but, lest your benevolence should render you anxious for my comfort in my present situation, I take the liberty to assure you that I am amply provided for.

I have no claim even upon your pity; but from my long experience of your tenderness, I presume to hope it will be extended to me. Oh, my mother, if you knew what the state of my mind is, and has been, for months past, you would surely compassionate my case! Could tears efface the stain, which I have brought upon my family, it would, long since have been washed away! But, alas, tears are vain; and vain is my bitter repentance! It cannot obliterate my crime, nor restore me to innocence and peace! In this life I have no ideas of happiness. These I have wholly resigned! The only hope which affords me any solace, is that of your forgiveness. If the deepest contrition can make an atonement; if the severest pains, both of body and mind, can restore me to your charity, you will not be inexorable! Oh, let my sufferings be deemed a sufficient punishment; and add not the insupportable weight of a parent's wrath! At present, I cannot see you. The effect of my crime is too obvious to be longer concealed, to elude the invidious eye of curiosity. This night, therefore, I leave your hospitable mansion! This night I become a wretched wanderer from thy paternal roof! Oh, that the grave were this night to be my lodging! Then should I lie down and be at rest! Trusting in the mercy of God, through the mediation of his son; I think I could meet my heavenly father with more composure and confidence, than my earthly parent!

Let not the faults and misfortunes of your daughter oppress your mind. Rather let the conviction of having faithfully discharged your duty to your lost child, support and console you in this trying scene.

Since I wrote the above, you have kindly granted me your for-

giveness, though you knew not how great, how aggravated was my offence! You forgive me, you say: Oh, the harmonious, the transporting sound! It has revived my drooping spirits; and will enable me to encounter, with resolution, the trials before me!

Farewell, my dear mamma! pity and pray for your ruined child; and be assured, that affection and gratitude will be the last sentiments, which expire in the breast of your repenting daughter,

ELIZA WHARTON.

LETTER LXIX.

TO MISS JULIA GRANBY.

TUESDAY.

My Dear Friend,

BY that endearing title you permit me still to address you, and such you have always proved yourself, by a participation of my distresses, as well as by the consoling voice of pity and forgiveness. What destiny Providence designs for me, I know not; but I have my forebodings that this is the last time I shall ever accost you! Nor does this apprehension arise merely from a disturbed imagination. I have reason to think myself in a confirmed consumption, which commonly proves fatal to persons in my situation. I have carefully concealed every complaint of the kind from my mamma, for fear of distressing her; yet I have never been insensible of their probable issue, and have bidden a sincere welcome to them, as the harbingers of my speedy release from a life of guilt and woe!

I am going from you, Julia. This night separates us, perhaps, for ever! I have not resolution to encounter the tears of my friends; and therefore seek shelter among strangers; where none

knows, or is interested in my melancholy story. The place of my seclusion I studiously conceal; yet I shall take measures that you may be apprized of my fate.

Should it please God to spare and restore me to health, I shall return, and endeavor, by a life of penitence and rectitude, to expiate my past offences. But should I be called from this scene of action; and leave behind me a helpless babe, the innocent sufferer of its mother's shame, Oh, Julia, let your friendship for me extend to the little stranger! Intercede with my mother to take it under her protection; and transfer to it all her affection for me; to train it up in the ways of piety and virtue, that it may compensate her for the afflictions which I have occasioned!

One thing more I have to request. Plead for me with my two best friends, Mrs. Richman and Mrs. Sumner. I ask you not to palliate my faults; that cannot be done; but to obtain, if possible, their forgiveness. I cannot write all my full mind suggests on this subject. You know the purport; and can better express it for me.

And now, my dear Julia, recommending myself again to your benevolence, to your charity and (may I add?) to your affection; and entreating that the fatal consequences of my folly, now fallen upon my devoted head, may suffice for my punishment; let me conjure you to bury my crimes in the grave with me, and to preserve the remembrance of my former virtues, which engaged your love and confidence; more especially of that ardent esteem for you, which will glow till the last expiring breath of your despairing

ELIZA WHARTON.

Letter LXX.

TO MR. CHARLES DEIGHTON.

HARTFORD.

I HAVE, at last, accomplished the removal of my darling girl, from a place where she thought every eye accused, and every heart condemned her.

She has become quite romantic in her notions. She would not permit me to accompany her, lest it should be reported that we had eloped together. I provided amply for her future exigencies, and conveyed her by night to the distance of ten or twelve miles, where we met the stage, in which I had previously secured her a seat. The agony of her grief at being thus obliged to leave her mother's house, baffles all description.

It very sensibly affected me, I know. I was almost a penitent. I am sure I acted like one, whether I were sincere or not. She chose to go where she was totally unknown. She would leave the stage, she said, before it reached Boston, and take passage in a more private carriage to Salem, or its vicinity, where she would fix her abode; chalking the initials of my name over the door, as a signal to me of her residence.

She is exceedingly depressed; and says she neither expects nor wishes to survive her lying in. Insanity, for aught I know, must be my lot, if she should die. But I will not harbor the idea. I hope, one time or other, to have the power to make her amends, even by marriage. My wife may be provoked, I imagine, to sue for a divorce. If she should, she would find no difficulty in obtaining it; and then I would take Eliza in her stead. Though I confess that the idea of being thus connected with a woman whom I have been able to dishonor would be rather hard to surmount. It would hurt even my delicacy, little as you may think me to possess, to have a wife whom I know to be seducible. And, on this

account, I cannot be positive that even Eliza would retain my love.

My Nancy and I have lived a pretty uncomfortable life, of late. She has been very suspicious of my amour with Eliza; and now and then expressed her jealous sentiments a little more warmly than my patience would bear. But the news of Eliza's circumstances and retirement, being publicly talked of, have reached her ears, and rendered her quite outrageous. She tells me she will no longer brook my indifference and infidelity; intends soon to return to her father's house, and extricate herself from me intirely. My general reply to all this, is, that she knew my character before we married, and could reasonably expect nothing less than what has happened. I shall not oppose her leaving me, as it may conduce to the execution of the plan I have hinted above.

To morrow I shall set out to visit my disconsolate fair one. From my very soul I pity her; and wish I could have preserved her virtue consistently with the indulgence of my passion. To her I lay not the principal blame, as in like cases, I do to the sex in general. My finesse was too well planned for detection, and my snares too deeply laid for any one to escape who had the least warmth in her constitution, or affection in her heart. I shall, therefore, be the less whimsical about a future connection, and the more solicitous to make her reparation, should it ever be in my power.

Her friends are all in arms about her. I dare say I have the imprecations of the whole fraternity. They may thank themselves in part; for I always swore revenge for their dislike and coldness towards me. Had they been politic, they would have conducted more like the aborigines of the country, who are said to worship the devil out of fear.

I am afraid I shall be obliged to remove my quarters; for Eliza was so great a favorite in town, that I am looked upon with an evil eye. I plead with her before we parted last, to forgive my seducing her; alledged my ardent love, and my inability to possess her in any other way. How, said she, can that be love which de-

stroys its object? But granting what you say, you have frustrated your own purpose. You have deprived yourself of my society, which might have been innocently enjoyed. You have cut me off from life in the midst of my days. You have rendered me the reproach of my friends, the disgrace of my family, and a dishonor to virtue and my sex! but I forgive you, added she. Yes, Sanford, I forgive you; and sincerely pray for your repentance and reformation. I hope to be the last wretched female, sacrificed by you to the arts of falsehood and seduction!

May my unhappy story serve as a beacon to warn the American fair of the dangerous tendency and destructive consequences of associating with men of your character, of destroying their time, and risking their reputation by the practice of coquetry and its attendant follies! But for these, I might have been honorably connected; and capable, at this moment, of diffusing and receiving happiness! But for your arts, I might have remained a blessing to society, as well as the delight and comfort of my friends!

Your being a married man unspeakably aggravates both your guilt and mine. This circumstance annexes indelible shame to our crime! You have rent asunder the tenderest ties of nature! You have broken the bonds of conjugal love, which ought ever to be kept sacred and inviolate! You have filled with grief and discontent the heart of your amiable wife, whom gratitude, if no other principle, should have induced you to cherish with tenderness; and I, wretch that I am, have been your accomplice!

But I cease to reproach you. You have acted but too consistently with the character, which I was sufficiently apprised you sustained. The blame then may be retorted on myself, for disregarding the counsels, warnings and admonitions of my best friends. You have prided yourself in the character of a libertine. Glory no longer in your shame! You have accomplished your designs; your dreadful designs against me! Let this suffice. Add not to the number of those deluded creatures, who will one day rise up in judgment against you, and condemn you.

By this time we had nearly reached the inn, and were soon to

part. I seized her hand and exclaimed, you must not leave me, Eliza, with that awful anathema on your lips! Oh, say that you will forget my past faults. That, said she, I shall soon do; for in the grave there is no remembrance! This to my mind, was a harsher sentence than the other; and almost threw me into despair. Never was I so wrought upon before! I knew not what to say or do! She saw my distress, and kindly softened her manner. If I am severe, said she, it is because I wish to impress your mind with such a sense of your offences against your Maker, your friends and society in general, as may effect your repentance and amendment. I wish not to be your accuser, but your reformer. On several accounts, I view my own crime in a more aggravated light than yours; but my conscience is awakened to a conviction of my guilt. Yours, I fear is not. Let me conjure you to return home, and endeavor by your future kindness and fidelity to your wife, to make her all the amends in your power. By a life of virtue and religion, you may yet become a valuable member of society, and secure happiness both here and hereafter.

I begged leave to visit her retirement next week, not in continuation of our amour, but as a friend, solicitous to know her situation and welfare. Unable to speak, she only bowed assent. The stage being now ready, I whispered some tender things in her ear, and kissing her cheek, which was all she would permit, suffered her to depart.

My body remains behind; but my soul, if I have any, went with her!

This was a horrid lecture, Charles! She brought every charge against me, which a fruitful and gloomy imagination could suggest! But I hope, when she recovers, she will resume her former cheerfulness, and become as kind and agreeable as ever. My anxiety for her safety is very great. I trust, however, it will soon be removed; and peace and pleasure be restored to your humble servant,

PETER SANFORD.

Letter LXXI.

TO MRS. LUCY SUMNER.

HARTFORD.

THE drama is now closed! A tragical one indeed it has proved!

How sincerely, my dear Mrs. Sumner, must the friends of our departed Eliza, sympathize with each other; and with her afflicted, bereaved parent!

You have doubtless seen the account, in the public papers, which gave us the melancholy intelligence. But I will give you a detail of circumstances.

A few days after my last was written, we heard that Major Sanford's property was attached, and he a prisoner in his own house. He was the last man, to whom we wished to apply for information respecting the forlorn wanderer; yet we had no other resource. And after waiting a fortnight in the most cruel suspense, we wrote a billet, entreating him, if possible, to give some intelligence concerning her. He replied, that he was unhappily deprived of all means of knowing himself; but hoped soon to relieve his own, and our anxiety about her.

In this situation we continued, till a neighbor (purposely, we since concluded) sent us a Boston paper. Mrs. Wharton took it, and inconscious of its contents, observed that the perusal might divert her, a few moments. She read for some time; when it suddenly dropped upon the floor. She clasped her hands together, and raising her streaming eyes to heaven, exclaimed, It is the Lord; let him do what he will! Be still, O my soul, and know that he is God!

What, madam, said I, can be the matter? She answered not; but with inexpressible anguish depicted in her countenance, pointed to the paper. I took it up, and soon found the fatal para-

graph. I shall not attempt to paint our heart felt grief and lamen-
tation upon this occasion; for we had no doubt of Eliza's being
the person described, as a stranger, who died at Danvers, last
July. Her delivery of a child; her dejected state of mind; the
marks upon her linen; indeed, every circumstance in the adver-
tisement convinced us beyond dispute that it could be no other.
Mrs. Wharton retired immediately to her chamber, where she
continued overwhelmed with sorrow that night and the follow-
ing day. Such, in fact, has been her habitual frame ever since;
though the endeavors of her friends, who have sought to con-
sole her, have rendered her somewhat more conversable. My tes-
timony of Eliza's penitence, before her departure, is a source of
comfort to this disconsolate parent. She fondly cherished the
idea, that having expiated her offence by sincere repentance and
amendment, her deluded child finally made a happy exchange
of worlds. But the desperate resolution, which she formed, and
executed of becoming a fugitive; of deserting her mother's house
and protection, and of wandering and dying among strangers, is
a most distressing reflection to her friends; especially to her
mother, in whose breast so many painful ideas arise, that she
finds it extremely difficult to compose herself to that resignation,
which she evidently strives to exemplify.

Eliza's brother has been to visit her last retreat; and to learn
the particulars of her melancholy exit. He relates, that she was
well accommodated, and had every attention and assistance,
which her situation required. The people where she resided ap-
pear to have a lively sense of her merit and misfortunes. They
testify her modest deportment, her fortitude under the suffer-
ings to which she was called, and the serenity and composure,
with which she bid a last adieu to the world. Mr. Wharton has
brought back several scraps of her writing, containing miscella-
neous reflections on her situation, the death of her babe, and the
absence of her friends. Some of these were written before, some
after her confinement. These valuable testimonies of the affect-
ing sense, and calm expectation she entertained of her approach-
ing dissolution, are calculated to sooth and comfort the minds of

mourning connections. They greatly alleviate the regret occa-
sioned by her absence, at this awful period.

Her elopement can be equalled only by the infatuation which
caused her ruin.

> "But let no one reproach her memory.
> Her life has paid the forfeit of her folly.
> Let that suffice."

I am told that Major Sanford is quite frantic. Sure I am that he
has reason to be. If the mischiefs he has brought upon others re-
turn upon his own head, dreadful indeed must be his portion!
His wife has left him, and returned to her parents. His estate,
which has been long mortgaged, is taken from him; and poverty
and disgrace await him! Heaven seldom leaves injured inno-
cence unavenged! Wretch, that he is, he ought for ever to be ban-
ished from human society! I shall continue with Mrs. Wharton,
till the lenient hand of time has assuaged her sorrows; and then
make my promised visit to you. I will bring Eliza's posthumous
papers with me, when I come to Boston, as I have not time to
copy them now.

I foresee, my dear Mrs. Sumner, that this disastrous affair will
suspend your enjoyments, as it has mine. But what are our feel-
ings, compared with the pangs which rend a parent's heart?
This parent, I here behold, inhumanly stripped of the best solace
of her declining years, by the ensnaring machinations of a profli-
gate debauchee! Not only the life, but what was still dearer, the
reputation and virtue of the unfortunate Eliza, have fallen vic-
tims at the shrine of *libertinism!* Detested be the epithet! Let it
henceforth bear its true signature, and candor itself shall call it
lust and *brutality!*

Execrable is the man, however arrayed in magnificence,
crowned with wealth, or decorated with the external graces and
accomplishments of fashionable life, who shall presume to dis-
play them, at the expense of virtue and innocence! Sacred
names! attended with real blessings; blessings too useful and im-
portant to be trifled away! My resentment at the base arts, which

must have been employed to complete the seduction of Eliza, I cannot suppress. I wish them to be exposed, and stamped with universal ignominy! Nor do I doubt but you will join with me in execrating the measures by which *we* have been robbed of so valuable a friend; and *society,* of so ornamental a member.　　I am, &c.

<div align="right">JULIA GRANBY.</div>

LETTER LXXII.

TO MR. CHARLES DEIGHTON.

<div align="right">HARTFORD.</div>

CONFUSION, horror and despair are the portion of your wretched, unhappy friend! Oh, Deighton, I am undone! Misery irremediable is my future lot! She is gone; yes, she is gone for ever! The darling of my soul, the centre of all my wishes and enjoyments is no more! Cruel fate has snatched her from me; and she is irretrievably lost! I rave, and then reflect: I reflect, and then rave! I have not patience to bear this calamity, nor power to remedy it! Where shall I fly from the upbraidings of my mind, which accuses me as the murderer of my Eliza? I would fly to death, and seek a refuge in the grave; but the forebodings of a retribution to come, I cannot away with! Oh, that I had seen her; that I had once more asked her forgiveness! But even that privilege, that consolation was denied me! The day on which I meant to visit her, most of my property was attached, and to secure the rest, I was obliged to shut my doors, and become a prisoner in my own house! High living, and old debts, incurred by extravagance, had reduced the fortune of my wife to very little, and I could not satisfy the clamorous demands of my creditors.

I would have given millions, had I possessed them, to have

been at liberty to see, and to have had power to preserve Eliza from death! But in vain was my anxiety; it could not relieve; it could not liberate me! When I first heard the dreadful tidings of her exit, I believe I acted like a madman! Indeed, I am little else now!

I have compounded with my creditors, and resigned the whole of my property.

Thus, that splendor and equipage, to secure which, I have sacrificed a virtuous woman, is taken from me; that poverty, the dread of which prevented my forming an honorable connection with an amiable and accomplished girl, the only one I ever loved, has fallen, with redoubled vengeance, upon my guilty head; and I must become a vagabond in the earth!

I shall fly my country as soon as possible; I shall go from every object which reminds me of my departed Eliza! But never, never shall I eradicate from my bosom the idea of her excellence; or the painful remembrance of the injuries I have done her! Her shade will perpetually haunt me! The image of her, as she appeared when mounting the carriage which conveyed her for ever from my sight, she waved her hand in token of a last adieu, will always be present to my imagination! The solemn counsel she gave me before we parted, never more to meet, will not cease to resound in my ears!

While my being is prolonged, I must feel the disgraceful, and torturing effects of my guilt in seducing her! How madly have I deprived her of happiness, of reputation, of life! Her friends, could they know the pangs of contrition, and the horror of conscience which attend me, would be amply revenged!

It is said, she quitted the world with composure and peace. Well she might! She had not that insupportable weight of iniquity, which sinks me to despair! She found consolation in that religion, which I have ridiculed as priestcraft and hypocrisy! But whether it be true, or false, would to heaven I could now enjoy the comforts, which its votaries evidently feel!

My wife has left me. As we lived together without love, we parted without regret.

Now, Charles, I am to bid you a long, perhaps, a last farewell. Where I shall roam in future, I neither know nor care; I shall go where the name of Sanford is unknown; and his person and sorrows unnoticed.

In this happy clime I have nothing to induce my stay. I have not money to support me with my profligate companions; nor have I any relish, at present, for their society. By the virtuous part of the community, I am shunned as the pest and bane of social enjoyment. In short I am debarred from every kind of happiness. If I look back, I recoil with horror from the black catalogue of vices, which have stained my past life, and reduced me to indigence and contempt. If I look forward, I shudder at the prospects which my foreboding mind presents to view, both in this and a coming world! This is a deplorable, yet just picture of myself! How totally the reverse of what I once appeared!

Let it warn you, my friend, to shun the dangerous paths which I have trodden, that you may never be involved in the hopeless ignominy and wretchedness of

PETER SANFORD.

LETTER LXXIII.

TO MISS JULIA GRANBY.

BOSTON.

A MELANCHOLY tale have you unfolded, my dear Julia; and tragic indeed is the concluding scene!

Is she then gone! gone in this most distressing manner! Have I lost my once loved friend; lost her in a way which I could never have conceived to be possible.

Our days of childhood were spent together in the same pursuits, in the same amusements. Our riper years encreased our

mutual affection, and maturer judgment most firmly cemented our friendship. Can I then calmly resign her to so severe a fate! Can I bear the idea of her being lost to honor, to fame, and to life! No; she shall still live in the heart of her faithful Lucy; whose experience of her numerous virtues and engaging qualities, has imprinted her image too deeply on the memory to be obliterated. However she may have erred, her sincere repentance is sufficient to restore her to charity.

Your letter gave me the first information of this awful event. I had taken a short excursion into the country, where I had not seen the papers; or if I had, paid little or no attention to them. By your directions I found the distressing narrative of her exit. The poignancy of my grief, and the unavailing lamentations which the intelligence excited, need no delineation. To scenes of this nature, you have been habituated in the mansion of sorrow, where you reside.

How sincerely I sympathize with the bereaved parent of the dear, deceased Eliza, I can feel, but have not power to express. Let it be her consolation, that her child is at rest. The resolution which carried this deluded wanderer thus far from her friends, and supported her through her various trials, is astonishing! Happy would it have been, had she exerted an equal degree of fortitude in repelling the first attacks upon her virtue! But she is no more; and heaven forbid that I should accuse or reproach her!

Yet, in what language shall I express my abhorrence of the monster, whose detestable arts have blasted one of the fairest flowers in creation? I leave him to God, and his own conscience! Already is he exposed in his true colors! Vengeance already begins to overtake him! His sordid mind must now suffer the deprivation of those sensual gratifications, beyond which he is incapable of enjoyment!

Upon your reflecting and steady mind, my dear Julia, I need not inculcate the lessons which may be drawn from this woefraught tale; but for the sake of my sex in general, I wish it engraved upon every heart, that virtue alone, independent of the trappings of wealth, the parade of equipage, and the adulation

of gallantry, can secure lasting felicity. From the melancholy story of Eliza Wharton, let the American fair learn to reject with disdain every insinuation derogatory to their true dignity and honor. Let them despise, and for ever banish the man, who can glory in the seduction of innocence and the ruin of reputation. To associate, is to approve; to approve, is to be betrayed!

I am, &c.

LUCY SUMNER.

LETTER LXXIV.

TO MRS. M. WHARTON.

BOSTON.

Dear Madam,

WE have paid the last tribute of respect to your beloved daughter. The day after my arrival, Mrs. Sumner proposed that we should visit the sad spot which contains the remains of our once amiable friend. The grave of Eliza Wharton, said she, shall not be unbedewed by the tears of friendship.

Yesterday we went accordingly, and were much pleased with the apparent sincerity of the people, in their assurances that every thing in their power had been done to render her situation comfortable. The minutest circumstances were faithfully related; and from the state of her mind, in her last hours, I think much comfort may be derived to her afflicted friends.

We spent a mournful hour, in the place where she is interred, and then returned to the inn, while Mrs. Sumner gave orders for a decent stone to be erected over her grave, with the following inscription:

"THIS HUMBLE STONE,

IN MEMORY OF

ELIZA WHARTON,

IS INSCRIBED BY HER WEEPING FRIENDS,
TO WHOM SHE ENDEARED HERSELF BY UNCOMMON
TENDERNESS AND AFFECTION.
ENDOWED WITH SUPERIOR ACQUIREMENTS,
SHE WAS STILL MORE DISTINQUISHED BY
HUMILITY AND BENEVOLENCE.
LET CANDOR THROW A VEIL OVER HER FRAILTIES,
FOR GREAT WAS HER CHARITY TO OTHERS.
SHE SUSTAINED THE LAST
PAINFUL SCENE, FAR FROM EVERY FRIEND;
AND EXHIBITED AN EXAMPLE
OF CALM RESIGNATION.
HER DEPARTURE WAS ON THE 25TH DAY OF
JULY, A.D.———,
IIN THE 37TH YEAR OF HER AGE,
AND THE TEARS OF STRANGERS WATERED HER
GRAVE."

I hope, madam, that you will derive satisfaction from these exertions of friendship, and that, united to the many other sources of consolation with which you are furnished, they may alleviate your grief; and while they leave the pleasing remembrance of her virtues, add the supporting persuasion, that your Eliza is happy.

I am, &c.

JULIA GRANBY.

F I N I S.